"What do I o?"

"Dinner."

Framed by the new flower beds, Lucas took Kathryn's breath away. The sunlight played on his hair and made deep shadows in his handsome features. "I meant for the plant and—"

"All I want is dinner…with you."

Aching with a deep unfamiliar yearning, Kathryn longed to throw her virtue aside and say she owed him dinner and breakfast. Instead, she said, "Dinner. Why not?"

She could argue that he was only a carpenter, he was not her type, he was a man she didn't really know…but she wanted him more than any man she'd ever known. And wanted him for more than his impressive body. He was downright wonderful.

"Carryout or real home-cooked meal?" Kathryn asked.

"Home-cooked, naturally." He smiled and linked his arm with hers.

They strolled toward the house—she in her sedate business dress and Lucas in his jeans and T-shirt. They were a unique—but hopeless—duo.

Dear Reader,

September is here again, bringing the end of summer—but not the end of relaxing hours spent with a good book. This month Silhouette brings you six new Romance novels that will fill your leisure hours with pleasure. And don't forget to see how Silhouette Books makes you a star!

First, Myrna Mackenzie continues the popular MAITLAND MATERNITY series with *A Very Special Delivery,* when Laura Maitland is swept off her feet on the way to the delivery room! Then we're off to DESTINY, TEXAS, where, in *This Kiss,* a former plain Jane returns home to teach the class heartthrob a thing or two about chemistry. Don't miss this second installment of Teresa Southwick's exciting series. Next, in *Cinderella After Midnight,* the first of Lilian Darcy's charming trilogy THE CINDERELLA CONSPIRACY, we go to a ball with "Lady Catrina"—who hasn't bargained on a handsome millionaire seeing through her disguise....

Whitney Bloom's dreams come true in DeAnna Talcott's *Marrying for a Mom,* when she marries the man she loves—even if only to keep custody of his daughter. In *Wed by a Will,* the conclusion of THE WEDDING LEGACY, reader favorite Cara Colter brings together a new family—and reunites us with other members. Then, a prim and proper businesswoman finds she wants a lot more from the carpenter who's remodeling her house than watertight windows in Gail Martin's delightful *Her Secret Longing.*

Be sure to return next month for Stella Bagwell's conclusion to MAITLAND MATERNITY and the start of a brand-new continuity—HAVING THE BOSS'S BABY! Beloved author Judy Christenberry launches this wonderful series with *When the Lights Went Out...* Don't miss any of next month's wonderful tales.

Happy reading!

Mary-Theresa Hussey

Mary-Theresa Hussey
Senior Editor

Please address questions and book requests to:
Silhouette Reader Service
U.S.: 3010 Walden Ave., P.O. Box 1325, Buffalo, NY 14269
Canadian: P.O. Box 609, Fort Erie, Ont. L2A 5X3

Her Secret Longing

GAIL MARTIN

SILHOUETTE *Romance*®

Published by Silhouette Books

America's Publisher of Contemporary Romance

To my brother, Dan, who fills my life with laughter and to Aunt Mary, who is 96, lives alone and wouldn't have it any other way—my inspiration for Grandma Brighton.

 SILHOUETTE BOOKS

ISBN 0-373-19545-1

HER SECRET LONGING

This edition published by arrangement with Harlequin Books S.A.

® and TM are trademarks of Harlequin Books S.A., used under license. Trademarks indicated with ® are registered in the United States Patent and Trademark Office, the Canadian Trade Marks Office and in other countries.

Visit Silhouette at www.eHarlequin.com

Printed in U.S.A.

Books by Gail Martin

Silhouette Romance

Her Secret Longing #1545

Steeple Hill Love Inspired

Upon a Midnight Clear #117
Secrets of the Heart #147

GAIL MARTIN

lives in front of her computer in Lathrup Village, Michigan, with her real-life hero, Bob. Growing up in nearby Madison Heights, Gail wrote poems and stories as a child. In her preteens she progressed to Nancy Drew-type mysteries and, in her teen years, to romance, where she often killed off her heroine at the dramatic ending. Many years passed before she learned what a "real" romance novel is all about.

Gail, also a Steeple Hill Love Inspired author, is multi-published in nonfiction and fiction with five novels, three novellas and many more to come. Besides writing, Gail enjoys singing, public speaking and presenting writers' workshops. She believes that God's gift of humor gets her through even the darkest moment and praises God for his blessings.

She loves to hear from her readers. Write to her at P.O. Box 760063, Lathrup Village, MI 48076.

SILHOUETTE MAKES YOU A STAR!
Feel like a star with Silhouette.
Look for the exciting details of our new contest inside all of these fabulous Silhouette novels:

Chapter One

"Not according to plan," Kathryn Palmer muttered.

She gritted her teeth and looked into the distance at the medium-blue pickup sitting in her driveway—a sure signal that she was late for her appointment. Being late was Kathryn's pet peeve, along with traffic jams…which is why she was late in the first place.

She stepped on the gas pedal, sending a spray of dust and dirt settling on the roadside foliage. Tooling into the driveway of her white-sided farmhouse, her tires skidded on the gravel. Her car came to a sliding halt beside the late-model truck, where inquisitive, deep-set eyes looked at her through the driver's window.

Intrigued by the blatant fixed stare, Kathryn sat a moment before pulling the key from the ignition. Rather presumptuous of the man to scrutinize his prospective employer, she thought, withdrawing the car key.

Greeted by the unbearable Michigan humidity, Kathryn's skin prickled as she pushed open the car door. It was only early May, and Kathryn wondered what the summer would hold. Unladylike perspiration formed beneath her jacket, rolled down her inner arm beneath the linen suit.

Her discomfort grew as she watched the carpenter step from his truck. Having envisioned an unkempt, beer-bellied laborer, she was thrown off-kilter by the neat, well-built man who approached her, his sage-green work shirt stretching across broad shoulders and tucked beneath his belt.

He flashed a broad grin graced by deep smile lines.

With a quiet chuckle, Kathryn noted the laborer's one imperfection. Fighting for recognition, an unruly tuft of sun-streaked hair jutted from his hairline like a young boy's. She extended her arm. "Sorry I'm late. I'm Kathryn Palmer."

"Lucas Tanner," he said, shaking her hand. He broke into an even-toothed grin. "The traffic, I know. It's a pain." His grin shifted from her face and followed a downward inspection as if she were the one needing remodeling.

Uncomfortable, Kathryn tugged at her suit jacket with her free hand and pulled it from her damp back. Extracting her fingers from his, she nodded and focused again on his face—not one drop of sweat anywhere on it.

As nonchalantly as possible, she brushed the beads that formed along her upper lip. "I moved to Metamora to escape the traffic. It was supposed to be my sanctuary from the city." She gave a defeated shrug.

A soft chuckle rose from his flat belly. "I hate it

myself. I think the sports arenas are the problem. It wasn't this bad when everything was in Detroit.''

Staring into the late-afternoon sun, he squinted, then shaded his glinting gray eyes. ''How far away do you work?''

''Southfield. I'm with a marketing firm.''

''Ahh,'' he said, and yanked open the truck's passenger door and snatched up a clipboard.

Seeing his readiness, Kathryn seized her attaché case from the seat. ''I suppose we can get started.''

''Unless you want to wait for your husband.''

Her chest tightened for a moment, and she wondered if he assumed women were incapable of handling business matters. The attitude permeated her firm. Slamming the door, she swallowed her frustration. ''That would be a long wait. I'm not married.''

''That makes two of us,'' he said, flashing a smile. ''Then, I'm ready if you are.'' He swung his clipboard toward the door as if indicating for her to lead the way.

She sashayed past his broad shoulders and unlocked the house, then motioned him inside.

Her irritation fading, pride filled her as she stepped in behind him and viewed her home. She loved its charm and unique nooks and crannies. And best of all, the place was hers.

On occasion she wondered why she'd bought a big old house in the first place. Her career was enough challenge. A husband and children to help fill the space was as distant in her thoughts as living in Tibet. But now things were different.

''Nice house.''

His voice pulled her from her musing. "Thanks," she said, following his admiring inspection.

Lucas tucked his fingers into his back pocket, tightening the denim across his backside. He meandered through the room, looking up at the high ceilings and crouching to eye the wide molding.

Since Kathryn had already noted the woodwork, she eyed his tight jeans, amazed. She then shrugged away her criticism. If the man wanted to wear trousers much too small for him, it was his business.

"This style is Adams," Lucas said, running his freed hand across the fireplace's white-painted mantel. He glanced at her over his shoulder.

"Right," she mumbled, not wanting the carpenter to think she wasn't educated. In honesty, she had no idea what style it was. When she bought the house, all she'd wanted was a chimney that didn't billow smoke when she built a fire. She admitted the fireplace was elegant.

Distracted by a scatter rug out of place, Kathryn bent and straightened it, lining it parallel to the door.

"Interesting," he said, turning full circle. "You weren't kidding about this baby. It is an old farmhouse."

Kathryn arched an eyebrow. "Did you think I lied?"

A deep-bellied chuckle rumbled from him. "No. But some people don't know a replica from a quality antique."

He raised the clipboard and began making notes. "You have a good eye for quality." Peering at her, he grinned. "And blue ones at that."

His audacious observation hit her like a brick, and

a humiliating heat rose up her neck. Her friend Amy, who'd recommended him, hadn't warned her about his boldness. Kathryn harnessed the desire to point dramatically toward the foyer, telling him to never darken her door again. Instead she wrestled with an appropriate, less dramatic comment, but faltered when she noticed his obvious stare. "Is something wrong?"

"No, but you look uncomfortable in that suit jacket," he said. "I can wait while you take it off."

Wanting to tell him where to get off, she felt her eyebrows shoot upward. Instead, the words bunched in her throat. Kathryn slipped off her linen jacket in silence while pinning him with narrowed eyes.

"Sorry," he said, obviously noting her displeasure. "This is your house. If you choose to wear your jacket, I guess it's your business." He shrugged and poked his fingers into his back pockets again, making a full pivot as he studied the room.

Comebacks about his tight jeans swirled in Kathryn's mind, but she kept quiet. She would put him in his place...if she decided to give him the job.

Then Kathryn realized the bad attitude might be hers. All he'd done was suggest she would be cooler without a jacket. Her co-worker, Amy, had said nothing about poor manners...although she'd mentioned something. Kathryn's memory failed her.

Lucas strode through the dining room archway, eyed it, then strutted into the kitchen. She followed him, gawking at how well he wore jeans and listening to the heels of his boots thud against the flooring.

"Look at the width of the mopboard," he said, looking up in the center of the room. "You don't see those very often."

She hadn't seen a set of shoulders like his very often, either, but she refused to lower herself to his banter. Instead, she peered at the chipped molding, noticing that it needed painting.

Kathryn agreed the house had charm, but his appreciation for the chipped molding and high ceilings seemed ridiculous. She pondered what else he would find enchanting...to impress her.

"That's a pity," he said.

Kathryn stifled her surprise. She followed his downward focus toward his boots and looked for a problem. "What's wrong?"

"This linoleum. I'd bet there's some fine hardwood underneath this. Maybe a puncheon floor."

"Puncheon floor?" she echoed, having no idea what it was and not caring.

He squatted. "Hard to tell," he said, running his fingers along the flooring surface. "Feel here." He beckoned her downward.

She took a staggered step backward, noting his trim hips and muscular thighs against the denim.

He lifted his gaze and beckoned her down.

Making the best of the situation, she closed the distance between her body and his snug jeans and leaned over, tapping the linoleum with her fingertips.

"No. Down," he said, gesturing his head toward the flooring. "Run your hand over here."

She crouched beside him, feeling ridiculous and wallowing in his spicy musk scent.

"Feel this." He grasped her hand and ran her fingers along the linoleum surface.

She felt nothing on the floor, only the warmth of his palm against her hand and the closeness of his body to hers. The nearness awakened an old longing she'd hoped to forget.

"We'll know better when I pull this up," he said, rapping his knuckles on the linoleum.

Pull it up? She gasped and rose like a missile. "I have no intention of pulling it up."

He shot upward and gaped at her. "If you want the kitchen remodeled—"

"It's not the kitchen...I have in mind."

Mortified, she eyed the too-high cabinets and old-fashioned countertop. "I suppose it could use some work," she muttered, then refocused in midthought. "I'm interested in redoing the back of the house."

How had she lost control of this interview? She pictured herself at work: delegating tasks, overseeing co-workers and preparing detailed reports. Today, she was as clear as pea soup.

He turned toward the farthest doorway. "You're looking for a laundry room?" He ran his fingers through the crown of his short, sandy-colored hair dragging them down to the nape, then lingered there, massaging the cords in his neck.

Kathryn cringed, hating his discerning eye and despising her lack of direction. "That's another idea...but I'd like something done with the summer kitchen and the enclosed back porch." Scrambling for a hint of executive authority, she marched past him, beckoning him to follow.

Since Kathryn bought the old house, besides wondering where her head had been, she also pondered how she could utilize this useless space. Now, as if her question had been answered, she'd found a purpose for it. Her grandmother.

She paused between the vast porch and the large summer kitchen, both in dire need of tender, loving care. "I'd almost considered having these rooms pulled off to add a large office area, but—"

"No, you couldn't do that."

She jolted at his forcible remark. "Well, I could," she said, not liking his tone, "because I own the place. I can do anything I want."

He faltered as if realizing he'd overstepped his boundaries, again. His tone softened. "But it would be a shame to ruin the structure's authenticity. The charm."

She eyed the thin, drab walls that caused her gas bill to soar during the winter months and shook her head. "Somehow I'm missing the charm."

His serious expression shifted to amusement. "Well, it's in the mind's eye. But it has potential."

"*Potential* is what I need." She rallied with her moment of wit. "I'd like these two rooms turned into living quarters for my grandmother."

His grin faded. "Grandmother? Is she ill?"

His sudden concern surprised her. "She's not ill," Kathryn said, "but she's getting up in years, and since my grandfather died, she's alone. She could use the company, and I could—"

She slammed her mouth closed. Why in the world was she about to tell this man that she was lonely sometimes? "So what do you think?"

"I suppose you'd need—" he turned a full circle, eyeing the area "—a bedroom, bath and sitting room for Granny, is that it?" He scanned the area, again. "Nice of you to take her in." Though his expression seemed sincere, humor flickered in his eyes. "But I'd suspect, after rambling around this place, Granny will give you some company.''

He'd noticed her faux pas. Heated frustration rose up Kathryn's neck, and she squinted. "Do you have a license?''

His forehead wrinkled in deep creases. "You mean journeyman's card?'' He reached into his back pocket, adding another measure of tension to the already cramped area. "Sure.''

She wondered if he could pull anything out of that pocket. Entranced again, she shifted her gaze. "I mean your *counseling* license.''

He withdrew his hand, letting it fall to his side empty. "Ahh...well spoken.'' He studied her a moment. Then, with a shake of his head, he continued. "Okay, so I got the picture. I'll stick to remodeling.''

"Thank you,'' she said with a huff.

He mulled over the rooms once more, then hoisted the clipboard and scribbled notes. "I see the summer kitchen working as a bedroom with enough space for a compact bathroom, right about here.'' His sweeping gesture defined the area.

With one fluid motion, he withdrew a giant-size tape measure clipped to his belt. "Grab an end,'' he said.

Amazed at his command, Kathryn stepped back. She was the boss in her house. But reining in her irritation, she followed his instructions while he measured.

Finished, he flicked the tape, and like a lizard's lightning-speed tongue, it vanished inside the metal container. Then, moving in one broad step, he poked at the wall. "Plumbing from the kitchen probably runs through here."

She nodded, noting that he definitely had a vivid imagination. She had no picture of how these grim surroundings could become a cozy bedroom and private bath.

Businesslike, he strode past her, his steps slapping against the planks. He stopped the middle of the room and stomped his foot. "Good pine flooring. By the way, I'll need to have your foundation inspected."

Wondering if her plan was a mistake, she sighed. After going through all this trouble, she had no idea if she could ever convince Grandma Brighton to move in.

"Although," he added, "from all I've seen, your foundation looks pretty good to me." His attention was directed at her legs. As his gaze inched upward, an amused grin danced across his lips.

She ignored his innuendo, assuming he was suffering from an excess of testosterone. "The foundation was inspected when I bought the house."

"It's for the building permit."

"But I'm not building. It's only remodeling," she reminded him.

Running his fingers through his hair, he shook his head. "Any remodeling needs a permit. Trust me."

His "trust me" set her on edge. And the project already seemed too complicated. She'd heard so many horror stories of single women being swindled by bogus contractors. She swallowed her growing concern.

Lucas hesitated. "Something's wrong."

"No, I'm having second thoughts."

Shrugging, he stuck the pencil in his pocket and

dropped the clipboard to his side. "You called me, remember?" His gaze pinned her to the spot.

"I'm sorry," she said, and immediately wondered why she had apologized to him. He was the one strutting around like a peacock in full show.

A hint of guilt nudged her. Wasn't she doing the same? She tallied it up to her lack of social life. She didn't trust the men at work. Their attention seemed aimed at getting her into bed or stealing her job.

Still, if she were honest, he intrigued her. But a carpenter? A match made in hell: his blue collar, her business suit. Who'd believe it? "So what do you suggest?"

Though he didn't respond verbally, he withdrew his stowed pencil, and she watched him draw a rough sketch of the floor plan. "You'll need new insulation in these rooms. I'll gut the old walls, but I'd like to salvage the original door and floor moldings."

He mumbled as he moved around the room, measuring openings and windows, then jotted down the data.

While he was occupied, Kathryn slipped into the kitchen to fill the coffeemaker. She needed something bracing to deal with her decision and her skittish emotions.

When she considered the entire situation, irritation sizzled up her spine. Why did *she* feel so responsible for her grandmother? Her sister, with her three kids, was in no position. And her parents had moved to Florida and left the whole worry about Grandma Brighton on her shoulders.

Then the problem of money flashed through her mind. While the carpenter listed insulation, gutting walls and installing a bathroom, Kathryn envisioned her savings sailing from her bank account into his pocket. But...the choice was hers. If she were going to make any headway convincing her grandmother to move in, she needed the rooms to be ready.

Before she returned to the porch, Lucas strode into the kitchen. "Mind if I sit at the table to do some calculations?"

She stared at his hand clutching the clipboard, fascinated by the sinew that traveled upward roping into the muscle of his forearm. Below his rolled-up long sleeves, his tanned arms were feathered with blond hair.

Realizing he was still waiting in the doorway, she mumbled, "Please, have a seat."

He withdrew a chair and folded his legs beneath the antique oak table, his fingers caressing the seasoned wood. "Nice," he muttered, "but it could use some good furniture oil."

She opened her mouth, but closed it again as she'd done so often since he arrived. Why argue with the man? The remark was probably a ploy to sell his handy-dandy furniture polish. If she had good sense, she'd send him on his way, but her good sense had taken a vacation. Instead, she compelled herself to be genial. "Would you like some coffee?"

"If you don't mind," he said, focusing on his notes. "Thanks. Black, no sugar." He pulled a small calculator from his shirt pocket and went to work.

Kathryn watched him, realizing he was the first man who'd sat at her table, other than her dad when her parents came to visit. Lucas's body seemed to crowd the space, and she couldn't take her eyes off the rippling muscles as he flexed his arm.

She pulled herself away and poured the brew into two mugs, then carried them to the table. She slipped one cup beside him and sank into a chair with the other.

Amy hadn't mentioned how handsome Lucas was. Instead she'd praised his workmanship. "Quality not quantity," Amy had said. Kathryn grinned, noting she'd finally remembered her co-worker's comment.

But the words slithered into her mind. Kathryn liked *quality*. But what had Amy meant by *quantity*? His voice drew her back.

"Did someone refer me?" He lifted his head, his forehead creased.

Wondering why he asked, she faltered. "I, um, you did some work for the Malones on Marywood Drive. I work with Amy."

"The Malones? Yes, I remodeled their kitchen." He laid the pencil on the table and folded his arms. "They were satisfied?"

"Satisfied? Yes. They, ah, gave me your name." His steady gaze pinioned her thoughts, and confusion plucked at her concentration. "She invited me over to see your work. You did an excellent job."

"Thanks," he said, picking up the pencil again.

Kathryn drew in a calming breath, freed from his puzzling gaze. The moment they'd met, she noticed a mischievous sparkle in his eyes. Whatever it meant, he made her uneasy. And she hated the feeling.

"So," he said, "you work with Amy Malone. Where was that, now?"

"Target Marketing." She hoped he was impressed.

Lucas leaned back in the chair with the mug between his hands and took a sip, his gaze riveted to hers. "And what do you do at Target Marketing? Telephone surveys?"

Her pride plummeted, and exasperation raced up her spine. Straightening her back, Kathryn lifted her shoulders to the occasion as well as her voice. "Telephone surveys?"

The same insufferable amusement leaped to his face. "I seem to have a knack for offending you." He replaced the mug on the table and leaned forward, folding his arms on the table edge. "I figured marketing involves surveys of some kind. I'd like to hear what you do."

Irritated, she spat out her response. "We research products and services through customer surveys...both by telephone and mailings. The results are studied and market strategies are developed, based on the results."

"And you are the...?"

"The director of marketing research."

"Very fitting position," he said.

If he was poking fun at her, she wasn't putting up with it. "Yes, and I got there by perseverance. Long hours, determination and drive." She gave him her most piercing look.

"Impressive," he said, unaffected by her visual knifing.

His one-word response ripped through her, and she shot him another look.

"I meant that," he said, humor missing from his face. "You obviously deserve the position. I know that working upward through the company ranks isn't easy.''

A ring of sincerity echoed in his voice. Kathryn mulled over his comment, wondering how a self-employed carpenter would know about company bureaucracy and the corporate ladder.

Sipping his coffee, he focused on his figures, and Kathryn returned the conversation to the business at hand, curious about the forms clipped to the board.

"So what's the estimate?"

He hovered over the paperwork momentarily before he spoke. "Rather than make a bad guess, let me draw up some plans and double-check prices. If you're interested in moving ahead, I'll have your foundation checked and make sure the electricity and plumbing are up to code."

What would he come up with next? "I assure you they are." She sensed another ploy. "I had that checked before I bought the house."

He gave her a sidelong glance, then continued. "Let me sketch some floor plans to scale, and I'll be in touch." He rose and slid the chair in place. "Shouldn't take more than a week." He extended his hand.

Kathryn rose and faced him eye to eye, guessing he was only a few inches taller than her five foot eight. Yet, she felt small and insignificant beside his solid frame. Clasping his powerful fingers, Kathryn felt her pulse escalate and tangle her brain. "You'll call me then?"

Following his agreeable nod, he headed for the foyer, then stepped through the doorway.

He slid into the pickup, leaned forward and closed the door, leaving only his silhouette in the setting sun. As he pulled away, he left her feeling more than alone.

Chapter Two

Lucas gazed through the rearview mirror at the large, shuttered structure fading into the dusty distance. Though he found the old farmhouse interesting, Kathryn intrigued him more. Even with her rigidity, he'd have to be a fool not to notice her good looks, the long dark-brown hair that brushed against her shoulders...and those intriguing deep-blue eyes that tried to anticipate his every move.

Beneath her controlled determination, he sensed vulnerability. He imagined she had struggled and worked hard to reach an executive position with her firm, and she seemed to have a difficult time backing off.

He considered his own situation. It was totally different. For most people, men or women, climbing to the top of the ladder was a struggle. But they didn't have a wealthy father who owned a successful corporation. A father who insisted his only heir take his rightful place in the business.

As if he'd been kicked in the solar plexus, Lucas released a mass of air from his lungs. Some people would give an arm or leg to be in his position. He hated it. Hated being duty bound to a father who'd been too busy to give him anything more than an allowance.

Yet, it wasn't his father, but his mother who made him duty bound. Months before she died, he'd promised to make amends, to rein in his free spirit and plop his rear end behind a desk.

In his gut he'd known his mother was too ill to last much longer. So he had promised. But he couldn't do it...not until he had no other choice.

No choice? He was thirty-five years old, fooling around with a word-of-mouth carpentry business and praying no one would connect the Tanner Construction Company with the carpenter, Lucas Tanner.

Kathryn Palmer hadn't made the connection, he was sure. She hadn't batted an eye. Like many customers, she'd most likely expected a grimy dude with a potbelly. He'd watched her peer at his hands, probably looking for dirty fingernails. He'd fooled her.

Fooled her? He'd made a *fool* of himself, acting like a Don Juan. He hadn't dated in a long time, at least, not someone who roused his male hormones. Without his family's money as incentive, women with substance steered clear of the self-employed carpenter who worked long hours.

He'd packed away any consideration of marriage years ago, when he became old enough to recognize his mother's dim, unfulfilled life. She lived in her husband's shadow, meeting his needs and keeping herself blinded to his father's drinking and carousing.

James Tanner lived fast and hard on easy street. Lucas Tanner wanted to live slow and easy.

Memories of his mother sifted through his mind. She raised him alone, determined to give him all that he needed to be a strong, self-directed man. And to his father's dismay, he was.

Lucas had no interest in being holed up in the corporate world. Yet, he had to keep his promise. His mother had been his family. No siblings, no father who loved him. Edith Tanner in her quiet way had made Lucas who he was.

The vision shifted from Edith Tanner to Kathryn Palmer. He saw no similarities in the two women. While Kathryn was outspoken, Edith was quiet. While Kathryn bound herself in business suits, Edith had always worn soft simple dresses. While Kathryn climbed to the top, Edith had descended into self-sacrifice.

He paused as his recollections shuffled along a new path. Perhaps they weren't totally different. When it came to dealing with Lucas, his mother had been determined. Listening to Kathryn, he sensed she was as calculated. Look what she was going through to help her grandmother. Then, remembering his mother's solitude, he thought he might have witnessed that in Kathryn, too. Tangled in her concern for her grandmother, Kathryn's fear was easy to recognize. The fear of loneliness.

Lucas could only imagine spending a winter rattling around that big old house. Creaking boards and flapping shingles could stir anyone's imagination. Kathryn's winters might be very lonely.

Lonely and lovely. When she slid from her sporty

automobile, he'd eyed her slender figure hidden beneath her royal-blue suit. In the late-spring heat, she
looked warm and uncomfortable. Curious, he longed
to see the soft woman beneath her business attire.

When he'd ignorantly suggested she take off her
jacket, he wanted to kick himself. Talk about chips
on shoulders, hers was a whole cord of wood, but he
didn't blame her. He'd stepped on her toes more than
once.

Yet, letting his imagination fly, he could picture her
in a sheer summer dress, something with a low neckline and short sleeves. Instead she was bound up in
layers: jacket, blouse and probably constricting un-
dergarments. She needed to be free. To breathe. He
chuckled, realizing he was echoing what he needed.

To Lucas, her suit was as binding and stiff as the
corporate rules and protocol he'd heard his father it-
erate. He feared the same rules edging into Kathryn.
But it was his own prison he feared, and, for his san-
ity, he was learning to live before he shackled himself
to paperwork and the stock market.

Time would tell with Kathryn Palmer. Given the
way he'd behaved, she might let him have the old
heave-ho before she even looked at his estimate.

He gazed into the dusk-swept sky, purple and pink
melting into the horizon, and envisioned Kathryn's
lovely face. He could picture her dressed in a gown
as soft and pastel as the twilight.

Kathryn stared into the refrigerator, hoping to spot
something that looked appetizing. Her mind was
clogged with her grandmother's absolute refusal to
listen to reason. She'd spent an hour after work trying

to talk some sense into a woman whom she loved dearly but whose neck she could wring without flinching.

Hearing Grandma Brighton's voice heighten in volume as she railed at her for even suggesting she sell her house made Kathryn grimace. "Sell this house?" her grandma had said. "Do you think I'm a mad woman? I've lived here more'n sixty years."

And she had. She and Gramps had moved into the small bungalow when they were young, shortly before Kathryn's mother was born. "But, Grandma," Kathryn said, hoping reason would strike her stubborn nature, "the farmhouse is too big for me. I'd love you to come...and I'm remodeling so you have privacy."

"Privacy? I have privacy right here in my own home. I love you dearly, Kathryn, but I'm not an invalid."

And that was that. Kathryn had pulled herself from beneath her grandmother's scorn and headed home.

Reliving their dialogue, Kathryn's heart sank to the pit of her empty stomach. What should she do now, cancel the remodeling or plow ahead, hoping that something would happen to change her grandmother's mind? At this point her effort was as useless as a lightbulb on a sunny day.

Kathryn's focus finally lit on the veggie drawer. Inside she spied a fresh head of lettuce. Then, plowing farther, she came upon a block of cheddar and ham slices. Chef's salad. With two eggs on to boil, she poured a tumbler of iced tea and wandered into the living room, sinking onto the sofa.

The deafening quiet wrapped around her, and she pushed herself up. She needed music, something soothing to block out her grandmother's frustrated voice. Shuffling through a stack of CDs, she slipped in a soft jazz disk. Surrounded by the gentle lilt of sax and bass, she returned to the kitchen and lowered the heat on the eggs.

Watching the water simmer, she questioned her motive. What had really prompted her to have Grandma Brighton move in? She contemplated her own loneliness, then her grandmother's solo life without her grandfather.

Maybe her motivation was a blend of reasons. She would enjoy companionship on a lonely evening. Lucas Tanner's comment stabbed through her thoughts. *After rambling around in this place, Granny will give you some company.* She balked at his comment, but he'd been right. Cold winter nights were isolated and endless.

Still, true concern niggled in her thoughts. Thinking of her grandmother being ill or falling with no one nearby settled in Kathryn's mind. Grandma Brighton was eighty-two, and though she was a spunky lady, everyone needed companionship.

She closed her eyes. Sometimes even she longed to have someone special in her life.... An unfamiliar image rose in her mind. She saw herself nestled in front of the blazing fireplace curled up on the sofa, her head on...someone's shoulder. *Someone's shoulder.* A spicy musk scent wafted through her memory.

She shook her head, startled at her hopeless musing. She was too old to dream about phantom lovers. She pulled back her shoulders. If she needed someone in her life, she'd have someone—that is, if her grandmother moved in.

Mingled with the music, a sound jangled Kathryn's thoughts. The doorbell. She snapped off the burner under the eggs and went to the door. Curious, she peeked through the small window. When Lucas Tanner's gaze caught hers through the glass, her pulse skipped.

She pulled open the door, feeling the pressing outdoor heat wash over her. "I wasn't expecting you," she said, unhappy with her rude-sounding words.

"I should have called," Lucas said, "but I was passing by and noticed your car in the driveway."

"Ah, I see." But she didn't see, because her senses were tangled in his manliness—the knit shirt stretching across his chest, the brawn of his arms, the faint scent of aftershave.

He studied her face, then chuckled. "Maybe you don't see." A captivating smile curved his generous mouth. "I figured we could set up an appointment."

"Appointment?" She pictured an inspector checking her footings or eyeballing her meters. "Appointment with whom?" she asked.

"With you. I'd planned to phone this evening, but since you're home, I figured we could set a time now."

At her firm, people telephoned first, then arranged appointments. "Come in," she said, feeling the heat creep into the foyer. "I'll check my appointment book."

She felt manipulated, and she didn't like it. Throughout the week she'd tried to push Lucas Tanner out of her mind and let reality fill his place. Was she ready to have this man, or any man for that matter, plow through her home—step into her quiet world—and then charge her for it?

With thoughts wavering, she widened the door, and Lucas stepped inside. In the living room she gestured toward the sofa. "Have a seat. I'll be right back."

She darted into the kitchen and placed the eggs in cold water, adjusted the pot holders on the rack, then hurried back to the foyer coat closet where she'd stashed her attaché case. She fumbled inside for her date book.

Before returning to the living room, Kathryn inspected her appearance in the antique hat rack mirror. She ran her fingers through her hair and glanced down at her ancient jeans and a baggy T-shirt. Who cared what she looked like? She shook her head at her vanity. The man was here for a job. She might hire him, not the reverse.

But in the doorway she faltered. Carpenter or not, he had stopped by to set a date to show her the floor plans, and she could be civil. "Would you like a cold drink?" she asked, placing her appointment book on a chair inside the doorway.

"Sure, if it's convenient."

She nodded and spun on her heel. In the kitchen Kathryn took a deep breath and filled a tumbler with iced tea, then returned to the living room.

"Nice music," he said as she handed him the drink, his fingers brushing against hers.

Distracted, she only nodded and sat across from him. Fighting for concentration, she flipped open her appointment book. "What did you have in mind?"

A lengthy pause drew her focus from the calendar.

"An appointment," he said, his grin playing havoc with her self-confidence and her pulse.

"I realize that." She lowered her eyes to control her distress. "I meant what *date* did you have in mind? When do you expect the plans to be completed?"

"They're finished."

"Finished?" Her head snapped upward. "So soon?"

"I'm fast." He sent her another toying look. "They're in the truck. I can go over them with you whenever you're free."

His unsettling gaze drifted from her face to her T-shirt. Discomfort rattled through her, and she eyed the clinging fabric, exposing her lack of a bra.

Kathryn folded her arms across her chest. "Let me be honest," she said, "I've run into a snag." As the words left her mouth, her stomach rumbled without mercy.

Lucas lowered his focus to the sound source.

She ignored him. "I've run into a brick wall with my grandmother. She's determined not to move...and I'm not sure if she'll ever change her mind."

"Hmm. 'The best laid plans of mice and men.'"

"Yes, but I worry about her. My folks live in Florida and my sister's in Ohio with her family. Three kids. I'm the only one—" She stopped in midsentence. "I'm sorry. You don't need to hear my problems."

"You're worried about her. I understand." He shifted forward on the cushion and rested his elbows on his knees. "Did you tell her what you've planned?"

His sympathetic expression burst her dam of frustration. "She wouldn't listen…even if I'd seen your plans and gave her full, glorious details."

"Did you explain she'd have privacy?"

"Yes. She said, and I quote, 'Privacy? I have privacy right here in my own home.'" Hearing the words again, Kathryn chuckled.

Lucas joined her. "Sounds like she'll be a hard nut to crack."

"Nut is right." Kathryn's stomach reverberated with a long, low rumble. She pressed her palm against the embarrassing noise.

He grinned and rose. "Listen, I haven't eaten, either. I'll call you later tonight. Since the plans are finished, you might as well see what I had in mind. Might give you some ammunition."

"I'd thought about strangling Grandma with my bare hands, but ammunition might work."

His eyes crinkled with his warm, wide smile. "Whatever you say. I want to make this easy for you."

Willing or not, Kathryn realized she liked this frank, amiable man and needed someone on her side.

"I'll make this easy for both of us," she said. "If you have time now, I'd like to see those plans."

"But what about your dinner?"

No matter what concerns she'd had previously, she threw wisdom out the door. "How would you like a big chef's salad?"

A big chef's salad.

Lucas stood beside his pickup and wondered why Kathryn was hard to read. One minute she gave him the evil eye and a growled retort, and the next minute she invited him to dinner. For one thing, she distrusted him. But why?

And was the construction job worth his time and his stress? He sensed it wasn't. Obviously, she was a taskmaster and probably a nitpicker, too. He knew she would be on his back. She definitely had expectations.

With a little discouragement he could sway her to forget the project. Tell her that Granny would never come to live in this rambling farmhouse. Or jack up the price. She would send him packing on a moment's notice.

Then, with encouragement, he could convince her that once Granny sees her own cozy apartment she'll move in. Why did he care?

Tugging open the truck door, he pulled out the roll of drawings and his clipboard, then closed the door and leaned against it. Why did he care? Because she was a carnival-mirror reflection of himself. In and under his corporate background, Lucas was a family man longing to live a simple, homey life without the pressures of big business. He wanted his own identity.

And Kathryn? She urged herself into the pressure-laden world of business. He guessed, like most people, she wanted to be loved and needed. Why else would she buy a big old farmhouse? True business entrepreneurs lived in no-work condos, city apartments or suburban ranch-style homes with lawn care services.

He'd been around executives too long not to see that Kathryn was like a lovely, softly rounded peg trying to fit into a complex trapezoid. Her eyes said it all.

Then he remembered her full, shapely mouth. When she smiled—which wasn't that often—her eyes sparkled, and today, even in her oversize sweatshirt, he couldn't help but notice her perky breasts, softly rounded and just enough.

Filling his lungs with fresh air and struggling to make his decision, he headed back to the house. But as he stepped toward the porch, a flash of a colorful wing caught his eye. Lucas paused and followed the flitting bird to a tree. Goldfinch. Like a magnet the bird drew him toward the backyard, and he ambled down the gravel driveway, searching the trees.

At a cylindrical thistle feeder, he spotted a purple finch, then a junco. He stood on the grass and surveyed the perfect habitat.

Noticing an outdoor recliner, he hunched into it and leaned back. What a life. If he'd been his father, he would have quit work long ago and taken time to enjoy himself. Instead, the aging man pushed himself from day to day through the stress and bureaucracy of a large company. And for what? For Lucas—who didn't want the wealth and the pressure at all. But Lucas faced the truth. Soon he had to take over and insist his father retire.

A robin fluttered into the birdbath, capturing his attention. Relaxing, Lucas pushed those thoughts aside and blew a stream of pent-up air from his lungs. She had quite a wildlife menagerie. His enjoyment of that idea made him realize he'd answered his own question. If Kathryn was willing to sign the contract, he'd take the job.

A loud tap caught his attention, and, turning his back to the birds, he caught Kathryn's curious face through the kitchen window, her knuckles rapping against the pane. In seconds she beckoned to him from the back door. He pulled himself up from the chair and took the old wooden steps to the enclosed porch.

"Sorry, I got waylaid by your feathered friends," he said, entering the back room and closing the door.

A faint scowl drifted across her face. "I couldn't figure out where you'd gone."

"Couldn't help myself. You have quite a variety."

"I do? I don't know a thing about birds, but they're pretty to watch through the window."

Pretty. More than birds fluttered through his mind. Kathryn's face had softened, and the stress he'd observed earlier had vanished. "You must know a little. I see you have a thistle feeder to attract the finches."

A faint grin appeared before she shrugged. "I asked about those yellow birds at the seed store, and the clerk told me what to buy." She motioned to the doorway. "We'll eat in the dining room." Before leading the way, she picked up the salad dressing and a basket of bread from the kitchen counter.

Lucas followed her, admiring the delicate sway of her hips and the bounce of her softly curled hair.

She'd set the table with two place mats, and he lowered himself into a chair behind one and waited while Kathryn unloaded the bottle and basket. Though salad wasn't what he considered a dinner, it sounded better than going hungry. But when she sat and handed him the large bowl, he was pleased to see much more than greens.

They remained quiet, each delving into their plates. He grabbed the crusty bread, scooping up the concoction and enjoying the meat and cheese. Finally Lucas lowered his fork. "It's good."

"Thanks," she said, sipping the tea, then lowering the tumbler. "So what did you bring me to look at?"

Before answering, he chewed and swallowed. "Two floor plans. Figured you'd like a couple of options. Both layout and cost."

"Sounds good, but I wish I weren't so uncertain. I hate for you to go through this and then—"

"Don't worry. It's part of the business," Lucas said, digging into the last forkful. He wiped his mouth and slid the plate to the side. "Let me show you what I have."

She rose and carried the dishes into the kitchen while he spread the floor plans on the table. Kathryn returned with a pitcher of iced tea and filled their glasses, then adjusted her chair.

"Pull your seat around here," Lucas said, his pulse sprinting as he shifted sideways to make room.

Without protest, Kathryn moved the chair and settled beside him. Studying the floor plan, she inadvertently brushed her arm against his. The touch sent his belly on a downward plunge, and he swallowed the sweet emotion.

The air was filled with her rich, heady fragrance, which prodded his senses and nudged him with familiarity.

Wrapped in her intoxicating scent, Lucas struggled to concentrate. Muddling along, he pointed to the details, the roomy bedroom closet and compact bath at the entrance to the old summer kitchen. With flexible insulation, new double-pane windows, and gypsum wallboard covered with paneling or treated for painting, he explained the cost could be kept to a minimum.

"I like this," Kathryn said, pointing to the second drawing. "What about the flooring?"

"Plywood covered with indoor-outdoor carpeting is less expensive and comfortable. I can lay oak parquet if you'd like, but that will cost you."

"I'll tell you what I really like," she said, lifting her gaze to his. "You have a private sitting room for Grandma, but I see an area that we can share."

"You have a nice yard." Suppressing his rattled hope, Lucas shifted his focus through the large bay window that revealed the expansive lawn. "I figured you'd like the idea. You can have breakfast there. Watch the birds. All you need is a garden."

"Garden?"

Her tone nudged him from the outdoor greenery to her amused gaze.

"A few vegetables and flowers," he explained.

She laughed. "Does that come with the remodeling?"

Her coy grin sent prickles down his back. "It could," he answered, wondering what in the world he meant. He had no intention of digging flower beds.

"Really?" Her color heightened. "I like flowers, but I don't know much about gardening."

For someone who seemed to have her thumb on the pulse of everything, Kathryn didn't claim to know much about anything Lucas thought important. He chuckled to himself. Kathryn, "the great," was missing out on a lot of life's pleasures.

He pulled his drifting thoughts back to the floor

plan. "So what do you say? Do you need time to look over the prints? Or—"

"No, I like this second floor plan. If I were sure Grandma would come, I wouldn't hesitate at all, except—" She hesitated, then arched an eyebrow. "How about cost?"

"I wondered when you'd ask," he said, watching her mouth curve into a smile.

He set the clipboard on top of the drawings, peered at the two completed estimates, then pulled out the one she'd chosen. "Okay, you want to know the damages."

Curious about her reaction, he sought her face as he flashed the final total. Pointing to the particular specifications and estimated costs, he heard a playful groan, but when he finished the details, she nodded.

"Then you want to sign the contract?" he asked.

Thoughtful, she nodded her head as if trying to validate her decision. "The construction ideas look great, but do you have any idea how to get Grandma here?" She raised her pleading gaze.

Lucas drew back, watching the tension return to her face. Worry knit her brows, and he felt dumbfounded as to what to say.

She released a deep sigh. "Either Grandma comes here or I'm afraid she'll have to go to a senior citizen facility eventually. I can't breathe easy with her alone in that house. She's feisty, but physically she's not able to keep up a house anymore."

Lucas grasped for words. Something to ease her mind. Anything to bring back her relaxed smile. "Once she sees what you're doing, she might like the idea." He paused waiting for her reaction.

She focused straight ahead, then a faint tinge of color washed across her cheek, like a bird's feathers brightening at the first hint of spring.

"Let me get started," Lucas suggested, "and then you can bring her home for a visit." He could almost hear Kathryn's mind whirring in thought.

"How long to complete the project?"

Lucas shrugged.

She scowled as if she'd never heard anyone give such a vague answer.

He couldn't snap off an answer. "It depends on a lot of things like scheduling the plumber, electrician, getting supplies. My guess is six or seven weeks. Maybe longer." Probably longer, his seasoned experience told him.

"Maybe longer?" she echoed, squinting, but her brows lifted with a challenge. "Then, the quicker, the better, I suppose." She fingered the contract. "So, where do we go from here?"

Her questioning gaze sent his salad on a Tilt-A-Whirl ride through his belly. Inside and out, the woman was beautiful. Anyone who cared about her grandmother as much as she did was a woman found only in dreams. *Where do we go from here?* A sly thought rose in his mind. He had no plans, but time would tell.

Chapter Three

Kathryn stared at the computer screen, attempting to concentrate on her work. Her thoughts, however, had sailed home, wondering about Lucas. What was he accomplishing today? After she'd given him a door key, she'd had second thoughts. He'd mumbled something about being unable to get to the house before she left in the morning, so to hand over a key seemed reasonable. But was it wise?

Kathryn had forgotten to ask Amy about her "quality and quantity" comment, but after seeing the plans and his price estimate, she figured she understood. For a reasonable fee, Lucas promised quality remodeling. She'd signed the contract. Now, would he deliver?

Kathryn tugged her mind back to her work, but the spreadsheet blurred again. She'd never have these survey results ready for tomorrow's meeting.

Disgruntled, she checked her wristwatch. If she ate an early lunch, maybe she could gear her energy back to her task. As she thought of energy, Lucas popped into her mind.

His energy level seemed different from most people's. One day he accomplished so much it shocked her. The next, she noticed no difference. And time wasn't standing still. She wanted those rooms ready.

After closing the computer program, she rose from her desk, tugged her shoulder bag from a drawer and headed for the staff lunchroom. When she stepped into the hallway, Amy hailed her from the end of the corridor.

"Lunch?" Amy called when she neared her.

Kathryn nodded.

"Let's go to the deli around the corner. What do you say?"

"Sounds good," Kathryn said, stepping into the elevator.

Kathryn followed Amy out of the lobby into the bright sunlight. Three buildings away they entered the cooler air of the deli. Once seated, Kathryn skimmed the menu, and when the order was taken, she settled back with her iced tea and fashioned her questions.

"I told you that Lucas Tanner is remodeling the back of the farmhouse, didn't I?" Kathryn asked.

Amy tore open a packet and stirred sugar into her tea. "You mentioned that he'd come to look at your place." She looked up from the glass. "Did you sign the contract?"

"Yes, last Thursday."

"You'll be pleased. He's filled with unique ideas."

Unique ideas? Kathryn had a few of her own...but first she sorted through the multiple issues running through her head. "How did you happen to contact him? I checked the telephone book. He's not listed."

"Because he's from Highland, I think. Bill's brother had some work done, and when we mentioned redoing the kitchen, he recommended Lucas." A frown settled on Amy's face. "Why? Is something wrong?"

"No, I just wondered. He works alone and no company name on his pickup. He's...very personable. His estimate was reasonable, and the week he's been there, everything's gone fairly well." She hesitated, recalling coming home to find a novel she was reading on the kitchen table. She was positive she'd left it in the living room.

"He's honest, Kathryn. Are you worried?"

Amy's voice faltered, and Kathryn felt a prickling of concern. What hadn't Amy told her?

"Lucas was...just a little slow," Amy said finally.

Kathryn's heart sank. If anything she didn't need slow. Besides needing the job finished for her grandmother, having Lucas hanging around the house week after week was more than Kathryn could bear. His sense of humor and good looks were growing on her. After he left each evening, the man lingered in her memory.

Mulling over Amy's comment, Kathryn felt confused and unsettled. "What do you mean by slow?"

"Not slow, exactly. He's easily distracted. I guess that's what I'd call it. One day I came home and he was sitting on the kitchen floor, thumbing through a gourmet cookbook."

"Cookbook? You're kidding."

"Another time, Bill nearly died when he walked

into the dining room and Lucas was sprawled out on the carpet. Bill thought he'd died or something."

Kathryn's pulse picked up speed. "Was he sick?"

Amy's face blossomed to a smile. "He told Bill he'd had a late night and decided to take a quick nap."

"Now that's weird." Kathryn's worst fears surfaced as she listened to Amy's explanation. What would she do if she arrived home to find him sleeping, sprawled out on her carpet? Or on her sofa? She moistened her dried lips, picturing the possibility.

"But he's meticulous in his work, and he's a nice guy. Just really laid-back."

"Laid-back?" The expression struck her as funny, and a laugh rose in her throat. "That's a little more than laid-back, Amy. That's 'laid-down.'"

After passing through Lake Orion and Oxford, Kathryn breathed a relieved sigh. The highway cleared. When she turned toward Metamora, trees lined the road's edge and the landscape rolled in stretches of farmland nestled between gentle hills.

Along the berm, wildflowers grew in colorful patches. Cornflowers, black-eyed Susans, and Queen Anne's lace bowed in the breeze and tilted their heads at passing vehicles. Despite the traffic, she loved a country atmosphere and loved her home.

Since Kathryn had signed the contract two weeks earlier, Lucas had taken care of the foundation inspection, gotten the building permit and, as of yesterday, framed in the bath, closet and porch area. He was ready to lay a plywood floor. If he kept up this pace, she'd be able to bring Grandma over for lunch on Saturday.

But since talking with Amy, Kathryn had faced some strange suspicions. One night she lay awake enveloped in the scent of Lucas's haunting aftershave. Her heart thudded as she almost sensed he was there with her. Bewildered, she remembered sitting bolt upright, snatching her bed pillow and burying her nose in the case. Now she wondered if he'd taken a nap there.

As she neared the house, Kathryn spied the pickup in the driveway. Confidence settled in, and she saw that Lucas was there and, hopefully, working. Yet, anxiety gave her a needling poke. She parked and hurried up the front stairs.

The past three days she'd heard the sounds of hammering, and today she expected the same. But instead silence met her ears. Her stomach slipped to her toes, and she stood motionless in the foyer. She envisioned his firm, muscular body lolled out asleep on the dining room carpet—or worse, her bed.

Tiptoeing through the empty living room, she paused in the archway, but Lucas wasn't sprawled there. Moving through the kitchen, she reached the back porch, thinking that at any moment she might hear him banging around in the summer kitchen. She hesitated, then barreled into the soon-to-be bedroom. Empty.

As she swung around, her search ended. Lucas sat shirtless on a lounger in the backyard, peering into the trees with binoculars. Her pulse leaped at the expansion of his bare shoulders and his nakedness. She shook her head, pushing back the unnatural emotions.

Quality, not quantity. Amy's words reared up to meet her. She swung open the back door and strode down the steps.

"Excuse me," she called, heading across the grass.

Lucas lowered the binoculars and pivoted his head in her direction. He pressed his finger against his lips to quiet her, and she froze in place. Who was this man to shush her in her own yard?

But as anger rolled up her spine, the ridiculousness of the situation flew to her lips. As she struggled with her grin, Lucas shot her a bright smile.

She strode to his side as her emotion rose again. When her gaze dropped below his smile to his bare torso, a ripple of embarrassed pleasure zapped her. His broad chest, covered with a vee of curling bronze hair, flexed with a ripple of hard muscle. She fought to avoid staring, but lost. Instead, she dug deep for a display of control. "Listen, what do you think—"

"Hush," he said, capturing her hand and sliding the binoculars into it. "Look near the top of that evergreen."

Her hand tingled at his touch, but she clutched the field glasses in her hand, refusing to put them to her eyes. "I don't want—"

"Hurry, you'll miss it," he said, rising. He tugged the glasses from her hand, stepped behind her and lifted them to her eyes.

"See it?" he said, his voice a breath in her ear.

Gooseflesh prickled down her arms. She lifted her shoulder to block the sensation that drifted to her chest and tickled her heart. Against her will, a giggle left her throat.

"What do you think?" he asked.

I think you're weird, flashed in her mind. "Give me a minute," she said aloud.

Holding her captive with his arms around her shoulders, she gave up the struggle and peered through the lenses he pressed against her eyes. Lifting her hands to hold them herself, she captured his fingers beneath hers.

He lingered a moment before he removed his hold, but he left his fingers curled around her shoulders, sending fire hotter than the sun down her limbs.

Flustered by her lack of control and inability to see the bird, she sighed. "Give me a hint," she said, after seeing nothing but unidentifiable swatches of green pine needles and blue sky.

"A cedar waxwing. See it?" His body pressed against her back as he lifted his hand and pointed. "There, it has a yellowish tail and a pale rust-colored belly."

At his words the bird moved in the branches, and she caught the flash of a bright-feathered bird about the size of a robin. "I see it."

She lowered the binoculars and swung around to face him. He stood a heartbeat away from her, and she swallowed to dispel the sizzle of emotion rising up her arms. "I see it, but what does the bird have to do with getting my rooms finished?"

"Why do you always smell so good?" he asked.

The question came out of nowhere and startled her. "Smell good?"

"Yes, good enough to eat." His gaze roamed her face.

"I suppose it's my cucumber and guava body lotion. You must be hungry." Her chest tightened.

"I bet I am," he said, his breath tickling her ear.

She sensed it coming and raised her hand to the soft fur of his chest, wanting to push him away, but she couldn't, her own longing peaking in the pit of her stomach.

His warm breath brushed against her lips as he drew her against him, then lowered his mouth with a tender, brief kiss tasting of summer heat.

Kathryn reeled back, her mind stumbling over itself. Why hadn't he been the grubby workman she'd anticipated instead of this attractive hunk of masculinity whose direct gaze made her weak in the knees? And how could she defend herself now? For during that fleeting moment, she'd welcomed his soft lips against hers.

She pulled up her shoulders and plastered a frown on her face. "Listen, I hired you to remodel my back end...I, mean, my house's back end, and... Never mind, what are you doing out here with your shirt off?" She demanded her eyes to focus anywhere but on his chest.

"Catching some rays." he said, a hint of amusement in his voice. "Even the lowliest peon gets a fifteen-minute break. Besides, I love to bird-watch. You should take time to—"

"Smell the flowers?" she snapped. "I've heard that before."

He chuckled. "That's good, too, but I was thinking 'take time to watch the birds.'"

"Oh," she said, wanting to hate him, but his face glowed with excitement over the stupid birds. Heat glowed on her cheeks, too, but for a totally different reason.

* * *

Lucas pulled the pickup into the condo parking lot and stepped out. He usually called his cousin before dropping by, but today he hadn't. This visit was spur-of-the-moment, and his purpose was unclear even in his own mind. But Jon was not only a relative, he'd been his long-time friend, and Lucas needed to talk.

He strode across the concrete toward the impressive Tudor-style building. When he reached the door, he rang the bell and waited, hoping Jon was in and not busy.

When the inner door swung back, Jon's smiling face answered Lucas's question.

"Look what the cat dragged in," Jon said, swinging the storm door wide and ushering Lucas inside. "Glad you stopped by. I've been thinking about you."

Jon clasped Lucas's shoulder and beckoned him into the living room. Lucas followed, always impressed by the smart decor that filled the room. Jon was pure class, good executive material.

The television flashed a Sunday pregame event, and Jon crossed the floor to lower the volume. While he had always been the spectator, Lucas had been the athlete.

"Sit. What's your pleasure? Wine, beer, cola?" Jon asked.

Lucas glanced at his wristwatch. "Cola would be great," Lucas said, plopping down into the lush brocade chair.

Jon headed through the doorway. Sitting alone, Lucas gathered his thoughts, his fingers tapping the broad chair arms. His mind whirred with feelings about Kathryn and questions about Tanner Construction. Since Jon was so much like Lucas's father, he'd always been a good sounding board.

When Jon's footsteps thumped against the terrazzo flooring, Lucas lifted his gaze. Though Jon's hair coloring was the same as his and they had similar features, Jon was taller and broader than Lucas, but not as toned. And Lucas noticed he'd gained some weight around the middle.

"I hope you don't mind that I dropped by without calling," Lucas said, already knowing the answer.

"You're welcome here anytime. So where have you been hiding?"

"Here and there," Lucas said, taking a long drink of the cola. "How's…how's my father?"

Jon nodded. "I should have guessed." A sad grin fell across his face. "He's okay, Lucas, but tired. He needs to get out of the business and take it easy."

Lucas stared at his shoes. "I know. That's what I'm struggling with." He lifted his face to his cousin's curious gaze. "I'd rather do anything than sit behind a desk, Jon. I'm a doer, not a planner. Not like you."

"You have a good mind. You're selling yourself short," Jon said, a scowl furrowing his brow.

"No, I'm selling myself *true*. I am who I am. I like being outside in the sun…or rain. I like seeing the floor plan turn into a room or a house."

"I've never gotten off on that," Jon said. "Give me a desk, credenza and a leather chair that leans way back." He tilted the plush recliner and lifted his feet.

"You should have been my father's son, Jon. You already have the last name."

"It's time to make amends with your father, Lucas. It's none of my business, but—"

"That's why I'm here, Jon. I'm doing my last job. An old farmhouse that I've grown to love, and…" He couldn't contain the smile that stole across his face.

Jon flipped the recliner forward and peered at him. "You've fallen in love with a farmhouse…or the owner?"

Jon knew him well. "A little of both, I suppose. I love the house and really like the owner."

"It's a woman, I assume."

Lucas chuckled. "I hope you know me well enough that no response is necessary."

"You old devil," Jon said. "I figured you'd be single forever. Now me, I've been playing the field for a long time, but I'm thinking about settling down."

"Congratulations. Colleen?"

Jon nodded. "So, tell me about this chick who's got you hot to trot."

Lucas shook his head. "She's not like that. She's different. A businesswoman. One of those hard-nosed, determined women driven to climb to the top, which she's already done. She's the director of marketing at a big firm in Southfield."

"I figured you for a whole different type, Lucas."

"Me, too. You'd have to meet her to understand. She's soft inside…sort of a paradox. For all her spit and polish, she dotes on her grandmother and cooks an occasional dinner for the carpenter."

"Carpenter?"

"Me. She doesn't know who I am."

"You're kidding." His expression shifted to doubtful. "She's yanking your chain, man. Everyone's heard of Tanner Construction."

"No, I'm sure she has no idea. I don't really think she'd care, but I'm testing her."

"You're what?"

"Testing, you know, giving it time. For once I'd like to know it's me she's cooking dinner for. Not my family's money."

"You're that serious about this dame?"

Lucas tensed. *Dame?* Not Kathryn. "She's gotten under my skin. She makes me laugh. Brings out the best in me. I like her, that's it."

A smirk covered Jon's face. "*Like* her. Come on. Who're you kidding? So what's she like in the sack?"

"I can't answer that," Lucas said, feeling a mixture of embarrassment and irritation.

"Can't or won't?"

"You heard me. Listen, Jon, you'd have to meet her. She's special."

"I'd say!"

Lucas swigged the cola. "Getting back to my real reason for dropping by—how about giving some thought to the situation with my father. You have allegiance to us both, I know. But I need your help. How can I keep the promise to my mother without being miserable the rest of my life?"

Jon let out a guffaw. "That's all you want, huh?"

Lucas shrugged. "Okay, so I'm looking for a miracle."

A miracle. Lucas longed for another miracle, one with soft, receptive lips, who would love him for himself. The miracle had shoulder-length brown hair that smelled like a summer orchard.

Chapter Four

"Can't see why you're dragging me out here to lunch, Kathryn," Ida Brighton said. "You usually take me to a restaurant. Gettin' cheap, are you?"

Kathryn looked toward heaven and groaned. "No, Grandma, I want you to see the house. I told you."

"How about photographs? You could just show me pictures. You live a dang-awful distance from civilization. I'm expecting to see cows in the middle of the road."

"You're being dramatic," Kathryn said, easing her tone to be pleasant.

Gazing at her petite grandmother, Kathryn sighed deeply. Muttered prayer had become her mainstay. Somehow she needed to convince this stubborn woman to give up her bungalow, once and for all. Patience had never been Kathryn's forte.

Her pulse skipped, seeing Lucas's pickup in the distance, and she hoped that he didn't have things in a mess. She'd been fighting dust and grime for weeks. Kathryn added that to her list of pet peeves. She liked things clean and neat. Everything in its place.

When she pulled into the driveway, she noticed the truck bed filled with insulation. She had to admit Lucas hadn't wasted time since the day she found him in the yard with the binoculars.

That day had continued to linger in her mind. Not the bird-watching and time-wasting part, but Lucas's broad chest and hard, powerful muscles flexing in the sunshine, his lips brushing against hers like a succulent peach fresh from the vine, all warm and tender.

Another morning she woke and pushed her face into the pillow, hoping to catch a remnant of his scent and imagining what it might be like to have him curled up at her side. Later that evening when she saw Lucas, hammer in hand, brawn bulging below his rolled sleeves, heat had risen up her neck. He hadn't noticed. She was grateful.

Kathryn stepped from the car and hurried around to the passenger door. The sports car was low and awkward for someone no longer agile. Knowing her grandmother, she'd be tugging at the handle, unwilling to have anyone give her a hand.

And she was right. When she opened the door, Grandma scowled. Rather than wrestle her, Kathryn stepped back and allowed her to exit the car on her own, but stayed close to lend a hand if necessary.

Watchful, she sent her grandmother up the three steps first. When they entered the foyer, the comforting sound of a hammer against wood echoed from the back of the house.

"Woodpecker?" Grandma asked, glowing with mischief.

"Sure thing, but my own variety," Kathryn said.

Grandma Brighton headed toward the rat-tat of the hammer, and Kathryn followed her, wondering if her grandmother's growl was part of her clowning. Kathryn's mother sent mixed messages, too.

She watched as the elderly woman gazed at the partitions, some covered with insulation. Without hesitation, her grandmother meandered into the old summer kitchen. With curiosity, Kathryn waited in the porch area and listened.

"You must be Grandma Brighton," she heard Lucas say.

"Grandma? I don't remember you as being kin."

Silence slithered from the room, and Kathryn grinned, imagining, for once, Lucas had been put in his place. But her grin faded to surprise when she heard her grandmother's next words.

"But you know, sonny, you're a pretty handsome young man. Wouldn't mind you being family. Not one bit. Go ahead and call me Grandma."

"Why, thank you," Lucas said, his voice echoing a smile. "You're a pretty handsome woman, yourself. A mite small, but big enough for all that counts, I'd say."

Ida giggled like a schoolgirl, and Kathryn stood gaping at the doorway, not believing that her grandmother would flirt with Lucas, as if she was a teenager.

Deciding to interrupt the humiliating conversation, Kathryn stepped into the room. Both heads turned.

"What do you think?" Kathryn asked, hoping to move the conversation to something more sensible.

"He's a real 'hunk,' I think that's what they call it," Grandma Brighton responded, her eyes twinkling.

Lucas's misty gray eyes smiled back at her, sending Kathryn's heart rocking on waves of confusion.

"I meant the *room*," Kathryn said, trying to keep the discomfort from her voice. "You're a tease, Grandma."

Her grandmother turned full circle, surveying the area. "He does good work, I'd say. I always thought this was wasted space." With a probing eye, she looked to Kathryn. "You'll use this as your new office?"

Kathryn hesitated, not knowing what to say that would do the least amount of damage. "Maybe, or a guest room." Her grandmother already knew this was a ploy, and as always she'd be as stubborn as a new puppy.

"Guest room, huh?" She pulled her spectacles from her nose, held them up for inspection, then slid them over her ears and peered around again. "I'm lookin' through a little grease, but I suppose it could make a nice guest room." Then she threw a broad smile to Lucas and winked. "Depends on who the guest is, I'd say."

Lucas gave a belly laugh, his smile as broad as Ida's, and Kathryn gazed at the two of them as if she were the outsider instead of him.

"I'll get lunch," Kathryn said, backing out the door.

"Hope you're settin' the table for three, Kathryn. You didn't tell me you had this charmer here. I might've come here without all my guff if you'd told me."

Kathryn escaped to the kitchen. Embarrassment rattled through her, and she cringed, wondering what Lucas thought of her flirtatious grandmother.

Amazed, Kathryn stood for a moment to collect herself. Her grandmother was eighty-plus. Kathryn had figured by age sixty those kinds of amorous, suggestive attitudes would be long forgotten. Today she'd learned something frightening. Would she be awake all night at sixty, sniffing her pillow and longing for romance?

Her head spinning, Kathryn listened to the distant hum of voices, curious about the conversation. She added dressing to the potato salad and pulled out the plate piled with thick ham slices. After putting a basket of sandwich rolls and condiments on the table, she arranged the rug in front of the sink and called them for lunch.

Kathryn had considered inviting Lucas to join them. But she'd hesitated, facing another uncomfortable reality. She couldn't get enough of him.

She swallowed away the uncomfortable truth. No matter what rambunctious hormonal feelings she had, her life was settled. She had no room for a lollygagging man to muddle her neat world.

Lucas's voice neared, and Kathryn paused until her grandmother sashayed through the doorway with him in tow.

When they were settled in the chairs, Kathryn passed around the bread and meat, then filled two glasses. The kettle whistled, and she poured boiling water into the teapot. Grandma liked her Darjeeling.

Once they were eating, Ida peered at Kathryn with lifted brows. "So, want to tell me why the porch has a partition? Leaves a person to wonder."

Kathryn felt her mouth droop, and she slammed it closed while her mind whirled for an answer.

"My idea," Lucas said, giving Grandma a wink.

"It was? And for what reason?" She lifted one brow. "Anyone put you up to it?" She sidled a glance at Kathryn and back to Lucas.

"Not a soul. Thought of it myself. Figured if your granddaughter decided to take in a boarder, the person would have a private sitting room."

Ida snorted. "A boarder? Now, there's an idea. If my granddaughter did that, she might get off my back."

Kathryn wanted to sink through the floor, but before she could stop her, the woman continued.

"How about you, young man? Wouldn't mind seeing you cozy yourself up in that room. In fact," she added, her face filled with mischief, "I wouldn't mind seeing you cozy up with my granddaughter. It'd give her something to do besides worry about me."

Kathryn slumped as deeply as she could in the hard wooden chair. Though her grandmother's words humiliated her, her own imagination heightened the feeling.

Lucas's smile reached his eyes, and he gave Grandma Brighton's shoulder a squeeze. "You know, for a sprightly woman with white hair, you have some pretty amazing ideas."

"How about some dessert?" Kathryn asked, her mouth still full of bread and meat.

They peered at her with a puzzled expression, as they still both clutched half a sandwich.

"I didn't mean now," Kathryn said. "I meant when you're finished." With no response from either of them, she concentrated on her potato salad, feeling as useless as a sprig of parsley at a truck stop.

Ida hushed and dug into her salad. Lucas took a bite of his sandwich, but his gaze bounced from the plate to Kathryn's heated face, and she cringed.

Observing Lucas with her grandmother was an eye-opener. Tender amusement seemed the man's style. He teased her, bantered with her, but with a gentle respect that contradicted his less-polished exterior.

Eventually he asked Grandma Brighton about her younger years, and Kathryn breathed a sigh, wishing she'd thought of that herself. It would have saved a lot of personal embarrassment.

Kathryn gave an occasional sidelong glance toward Lucas, his muscled thigh stretched below the table. The sinew tightened in his neck and flexed in his shoulder as he lifted the fork.

She envisioned the day he first strutted through her living room, his jeans outlining his strapping, masculine frame. How often had she looked at the men passing her at the office, shedding their suit coats and flaunting their less-than-toned muscles? She could handle that, but not this vibrant man who could so easily love her and leave her—like Bill Jeffers, her college steady whom she'd mistakenly trusted and loved. Until Lucas completed the renovation job, she had to control herself.

Finishing his meal, Lucas refused dessert and returned to his work. Kathryn fumbled through unin-

teresting conversation, hoping to keep her grandmother focused on something other than Lucas.

After a respectable visit, Kathryn suggested they
leave before the heavy traffic—which was a laugh.
No time was traffic light, since the Detroit population
had decided to turn the countryside into a suburban
Mecca.

At Kathryn's suggestion, her grandmother rose as
an ominous rumble rolled through the heavens.
Through the window, Kathryn spied a flash of lightning zigzag across the darkening sky. Without warning, a gale-like wind whipped the treetops, and Kathryn hesitated, wondering if they should leave the
house due to the coming summer storm. "Grandma,
maybe you should sleep here tonight."

"Don't like being a prisoner, Kathryn. I'd rather
get home," Ida said, hanging her pocketbook over her
thin arm.

Lucas stepped through the dining room archway.
"Looks like a bad storm."

"I know," Kathryn said, "I wanted Grandma to
stay, but—"

"You two!" Ida rested a fist on her hip. "You're
worse than a bunch of old ladies, worrying. What?
You think lightning will strike me?"

Kathryn shook her head and snatched her shoulder
bag from the table. "Lock up if you leave before I'm
back," she said to Lucas, then guided her grandmother to the front. The yellow-tinted air rolled into
the foyer through the open front door.

Kathryn dashed forward, but her grandmother was
one step ahead of her. The older woman pushed
against the screen, and the wind caught the wooden

frame, flinging it wide. Her grandmother tumbled down the wooden stairs.

When Lucas heard Kathryn's scream, he bounded from the back, charged down the hallway and darted past Kathryn as she stood frozen in the doorway.

As he leaped down the three steps, the gray-haired woman lay crumpled at the bottom. Lucas tensed with fear. Had she broken her neck? Was she alive?

"Grandma!" Kathryn followed behind him, calling her grandmother through her tears. "Is she all right?" she asked, her voice strident and trembling.

A moan rumbled from the woman's mouth, and Lucas knelt beside her as scattered raindrops hit the walkway, sending up a pungent smell of damp dust and grit.

"Call 911, Kathryn," Lucas snapped. "She's coming around but we can't take chances. Not at her age."

Kathryn vanished, and Lucas knelt closer to the woman, praying she wasn't injured seriously.

"What happened?" she asked, her face glazed with confusion.

"You fell coming out the door," he said.

"The wind. I remember. It jerked me out of the house." She shifted and released a heartrending groan.

"What hurts?" Lucas asked.

"Everything." She struggled to push against the ground for support. "Help me up. Use those big muscles for something."

"Lie still. Don't move."

Instead of fighting, she did as he told her. Pain washed over her face, and he nestled her head on his hand, amazed at how one second can change a life-time. Astounded at his rising emotion, unbidden tears pushed against Lucas's eyes. Except when his mother died, how many years had it been since he'd cried for anyone?

Though Lucas tried to calm her, Kathryn paced in the emergency waiting room with uncontrollable frustration.

"The X-rays take time," he said. "Pacing isn't going to help. Try to relax."

"Easy for you to say. She's not your grandmother."

"No, but I like her." The remark cut him.

She stopped in midtrack and faced him, her straight dark brows accentuating her sad eyes. "I'm sorry, Lucas. You've been nothing but kind, and I'm taking my frustration out on you." She covered her face.

"It was the wind, Kathryn. You didn't do anything wrong. And remember, you asked her to spend the night." He wanted to comfort her, hold her in his arms, but he couldn't. He was nothing to her. He'd told her nothing about himself, and if she knew the facts, she would feel deceived. To her he was a carpenter, nothing more.

She dropped her hands from her tear-stained face.

Lucas captured her arm and drew her to the chair beside him. "You can't blame yourself."

"But I do," she said, sinking into the vinyl cushion. "I should have been ahead of her to hold the door. She got away from me."

A quiet chuckle rose in his throat. "I don't mean to laugh, but I've only known your grandmother for a few hours, and already I see that she does what she wants.''

A faint smile rose to Kathryn's lips and she nodded. "You're right. She's worse than a two-year-old. You can give them time-out, if necessary, or send them to bed.''

"Or a good paddling,'' he added, watching her sad eyes glint with his teasing.

"Right. But Grandma, she's impossible.''

"Impossible, but lovable. You love her a lot. I see it even in your frustration. I envy that.''

Looking puzzled, she frowned. "Envy what?''

"The warm, loving relationship with your family.'' He recalled his father caught up in a world of money and investments and his mother a prisoner of it.

Kathryn gazed at him without speaking, a frown growing on her face. "You have no family?'' she asked finally.

"No, my father's living. We're not close.'' He felt a tightness grow in his chest, a longing that things were different between them. He'd felt it for years.

"Oh.'' Her gaze clung to his until she relaxed against the seat cushion. "I'm sorry.''

Feeling her flesh pressed against his on the armrest, he gave her forearm a gentle pat to let her know he was all right.

"Family of Ida Brighton,'' a voice bellowed.

Kathryn leaped at the intruding voice and headed toward the doctor standing in the doorway. He met her halfway, then led her into the corridor.

Lucas remained seated and watched Kathryn move outside the doorway, her long thick hair waving loosely on her shoulders. Her shapely body tensed as she listened to the doctor, and she nodded, glancing at Lucas for a moment before turning her attention back to the physician.

Lucas's mind whirled with her "on-again off-again" personality. He never knew what to expect. She reminded him of a beautiful, long-furred cat, spitting and clawing one minute, then purring in his lap the next. A cat, yes. *Kat*. A perfect nickname. He grinned.

Finally she stepped toward him, her long fingers knotted around the strap of her shoulder bag, her face filled with deep concern.

"What is it?" Lucas asked, rising to meet her.

"She broke her hip. They'll do surgery in the morning." Tears glistened on her lashes. "I hate to call my folks. They'll be so upset."

"Why not wait until she's out of surgery," he suggested. "Tomorrow. It'll be easier then."

She stared at the floor. "You don't know my parents," she said.

"Sounds like you do."

She gave him a lazy nod.

Lucas touched her arm, and she lifted her gaze to his. "Will you see her before you go?"

"They're moving her to a room. I want to see her to make sure she's comfortable. I'll call my parents after I know she's settled."

She lowered her head as if thinking. "Listen," she said, "you go on your way. I've kept you long enough. It's getting late."

"You're kidding." What did she expect him to do, leave her there with no way to get home? "I'll wait. It's no problem."

Her face filled with concern. "But—"

"But nothing. I'll wait."

She didn't argue. Instead she sank into the chair and rested her head against the seat back. Sitting silently beside her, Lucas had all he could do to keep his hands folded in his lap. He longed to soothe her with gentle ministrations, knead the strain from her shoulders and neck.

"I suppose that's one problem solved," she said after minutes of silence.

"Which problem?"

"Grandma coming to stay. She has no choice now."

"Funny how problems are solved," he said. "Not always as you'd expect."

"And now, I feel guilty as sin." She tilted her head and gazed at him beneath her half-closed eyelids.

"Guilty?" A foolish thought stirred in him. "Did you push her?"

"No, don't be foolish," Kathryn said, half frowning and half grinning.

"Well then, why do you feel guilty?"

The faint grin vanished to somberness. "I prayed so hard something would happen to stop her from fighting me that I wished her into the hospital."

Contemplating her heartrending expression, he couldn't control his chuckle. He placed his hand on hers, resting on the chair arm. "Look at me."

Slowly she raised her gaze to his.

"You can't pray someone into the hospital. You asked for a solution and got it."

"I know," she moaned. "Now the problem's not only mine but yours. I need that room ready when she comes home. No goofing off. You'll really have to hurry.''

"I'll see what I can do." His mind whirled with arrangements he needed to make. The electrician, plumber, the wallboard, painting, flooring. Too much in a few days. No way unless he worked day and night.

"Promise you won't waste time watching birds.''

Her pitiful grin melted his heart. He squeezed her arm, then lifted his finger and crossed it over his chest. "Promise. And don't pray about this, okay? God knows you'll have me in a sling.''

She laughed out loud for the first time all day, then poked him in the breastbone with a strength he'd never expected from a lovely woman like Kathryn. *Kat.*

Kathryn hurried into the house, pleased to see Lucas working on a Sunday. As soon as she closed the door, he came from the porch and met her in the kitchen.

"How is she?" he asked.

"Sleeping when I left. They told me she'd be that way until tomorrow, so I figured I'd come home.''

"Everything's okay, though?"

She eyed him, surprised at how sincerely concerned he seemed to be. "The surgery went well.''

"Good. I'm glad." He leaned his back against the doorjamb, his thumbs tucked into belt loops. "I suppose you're exhausted.''

"I didn't sleep well last night. Now I have to call my parents and go through it all again." She slid her bag from her shoulder and dropped it into a chair, then closed her eyes and rubbed her temples.

"Why not get it over with? I'll grab a pillow while you stretch out on the living room sofa. Then you can give them a call, and I'll make you a cup of tea." He vanished through the doorway.

She stared after him, his words filling her mind. Tea? Pillow? Had he really borrowed her pillow? The subtle scent enveloped her memory. She sank into the sofa, shifted sideways and raised her feet.

In a moment he returned with a bedroom pillow. "This one was handy. I hope it's okay."

"It's fine," she said, lifting her head and letting him slip the pillow beneath it. For a moment he stood behind her without moving, then drew his hand over her hair and slid his fingers to her temple, circling in a gentle motion. "Feel good?"

A slow, easy wave of gratitude washed over her while a grateful sigh slid from her throat. "Mmm-hmm," she said, her eyes closed. Too soon, his soft ministration ended, but before she opened her eyes, he'd shifted to her side and sat on the edge of the sofa beside her, tenderly rotating his fingertips on her temple.

She reveled in his touch and attention, her mind soaring to visions she struggled to control. Then, as if he heard her thoughts, he leaned forward caressing her cheek with his, his breath brushing against her lips.

Her heart skipped, and she feared he'd feel the excitement that overflowed her senses. Yet wisdom cautioned her to reject his advances, but her heart tangled around her words. When he shifted and guided his pliant lips to hers, she yielded while shivers of yearning rolled down her spine. Arching her back, she longed to experience more than his kisses, yet the warning alarm of her virtue charged through her again—and probably would forever.

Lucas lingered for a moment, his finger playing against her pulsing lips, then moved upward to ply tender caresses to her forehead.

He straightened and clasped the hand she'd pressed to her pounding heart, touching his lips to her palm.

"I'll get your tea," he said, rising, his voice husky and soft.

She inched open her eyes, wanting to call him back, wanting to throw away her years of chastity that had caused her so much sorrow during college. She'd felt so alone then.

She pushed the memories aside and watched Lucas vanish around the corner. Harnessing her wild emotions, she grasped the telephone and punched in her parents' number.

She had to admit Lucas had been right about getting the telephone call off her mind. Today she was able to ease her mother's fears with the news of successful surgery and a good prognosis. "I'll bring Grandma here when she's released, Mom. I have a carpenter renovating that old summer kitchen into a bedroom and bath."

A carpenter. Kathryn's lips ached from his touch while the words burned in her throat. What was she doing? Her good sense had vanished.

Her mother's voice rose in concern over the cost, and she calmed her again.

"Don't worry about my money. I want to do this.

Grandma will have her own sitting room. It's really cozy, and I can keep an eye on her. I'd hoped to convince her to move here, anyway.''

As she listened to her mother's lecture about finding a husband and having a family of her own, Lucas ambled in, looking at home and comfortable. Her imagination drew him back to her arms.

He set the fragrant brew on the table beside her and stretched out in the recliner with a cup of his own, his green T-shirt evoking visions of meadows of spring grass and wildflowers.

Kathryn wished he wasn't there to distract her...or hear her conversation. The response to her mother stuck in her throat until she gave in.

''Look, Mother, if I'd wanted to get married I would have done it long ago.'' Her gaze shifted to Lucas. ''I'm happy the way I am. And I'm too settled now. I don't need children to fulfill my life. Trust me.''

She closed her eyes, afraid of what Lucas might see. But the temptation was too much, and she sidled a glance.

He was staring through the window as if lost in his own world. But she knew she wouldn't be that lucky. Finally she appeased her mother and said goodbye.

''Aren't parents odd?'' Lucas said, his focus still out the window.

''What do you mean?'' she asked, agreeing, but uncertain what he meant.

''They always seem to know what's best for their children whether they're one, twenty-one or thirty-five.'' He turned from the window and settled on her. ''Amazing how they're totally wrong.''

"It is," she said, wondering if that was his age. "You're thirty-five?"

Lucas nodded.

Like a shield she grasped a negative consideration. Shouldn't he be settled at thirty-five? She already had success at thirty, with a good job and a lovely home. A prosperous woman like her didn't need a man.... "My mom thinks marriage is the only way to live."

"Isn't it?" he asked.

His comment surprised her. Confused, she faltered. "But you're not married."

"Not yet." His tone edged with question, and he leaned forward. "I think you're fooling yourself. You said you're happy being single, but my perception sees a woman who loves family."

Tension knotted in her shoulders. She had enough problems with her mother. No way would she allow him to speculate about her needs and wants, riling her emotions and giving her useless hopes. "You're a carpenter, not a psychologist."

"That's the second time you said that to me."

His sentence smacked her with the truth. Yet, if he knew so much about relationships, why was he single? Sensing his edginess, she picked up the hot mug and sipped it gingerly. "Thanks for the tea."

"You're welcome." His deep sigh filled the air, and he rose. "I'd better go. I've contacted the plumber. He should be here tomorrow. I'll make sure he gets in." His voice was serious with business.

"Thanks." He was upset, but she couldn't apologize. She had to protect herself. Every day he grew closer, and she became weaker.

After he bolted from the room, she closed her eyelids, knowing she'd been cruel. He'd done so much for her, and she hadn't shown him any kindness the past few hours. He had the right to his opinion...even if it was wrong.

She heard the back door slam and waited for the truck to pull away. But she heard nothing.

Finally her curiosity won out and she opened the door. Lucas was bending beneath the hood of the pickup, his shoulders hunched.

"Something wrong?" she called.

He shot her a look, then turned his head back toward the engine.

She waited.

Finally he slammed the hood, turned and tromped up the stairs. "May I use your telephone?"

His face was tense, and irritation sparked in his voice. She stepped aside as he strode past her.

"What's the problem?" she called after him while concern wavered through her.

He didn't answer.

From the kitchen she heard him speaking on the telephone. With a slam of the receiver he marched back into the living room. "I'm sure it's the transmission. It's been acting up, and I kept pressing my luck. I called a tow truck."

She searched his face praying to see the appearance of his usual good-natured smile. "Lucas, I'm sorry I was rude. Sometimes I'm—"

"A snob," he said. "My father can be a snob."

Snob? "Is that what you think?"

"At times," he said. "Do you realize we have a problem?"

Her heart lurched. Would he refuse to finish the job? "Problem? How?"

"If my truck's tied up, I'm going to have difficulty getting this job done. I can call my cousin or rent a car, arrange deliveries by truck, I suppose, but—"

Sorrow washed over her. She'd treated him terribly, trying to control her rampant emotions...which weren't his fault but her own.

"We'll work something out, Lucas." Her ears rang with her words, and her stomach plummeted to her toes. How much more could she handle? Between her mother's nagging, Grandma Brighton's surgery, her house covered with dust and now...these constant, erotic feelings tingled through her.

"Work what out?" he asked, his arms dangling at his side with helplessness.

"Let them tow the truck to the garage tonight. I'd decided to take off tomorrow, anyway. You know, to spend time with my grandmother. We can see about the pickup then."

"So explain yourself, Kat," he said, closing the distance between them. He tilted her chin upward.

"'Kat'? Why—"

"It's a perfect name," he said, his face mellowing. Lucas's eyes searched hers. "So tell me, Kat, how does that work things out for me?"

Her heart lurched, then galloped across her chest. She caught her breath before she whispered the words that had risen earlier in her thoughts. "Lucas, you can spend the night here."

Chapter Five

Sitting in her car in front of the repair garage, Kathryn waited while Lucas watched the driver release his pickup from the tow truck. In this "auto shop" realm, Lucas seemed in command while she felt useless. She hated the feeling, and the car provided a hideout.

She hadn't caught her breath since she'd opened her mouth and invited Lucas to spend the night. What was she thinking?

The flagrant images that had entered her mind the past week shamed her. She gazed outside at Lucas standing with his hands tucked in his back pockets, his jeans nestled around his firm legs, his corded arm muscles.

Inviting Lucas to stay was like dropping a baited hook in the water and hoping not to catch a fish. Senseless. But that's what she had done.

Dealing with men in the business world had only validated Kathryn's belief that the only thing most men wanted in a woman was a homemaker and bed partner. And the latter didn't necessarily include marriage.

She closed her eyes a moment, searching for a truer reality. Maybe she was wrong. Her past had dampened her faith in men. Bill Jeffers rose in her mind.

The old hurt and humiliation knifed through her. She had a career. That's all she needed. She could never take the chance on loving again. Men were driven by urges and hormones. She would cling to her intelligence.

While her deliberation reflected her belief, her focus riveted on Lucas. He was an exceptional specimen. And though so often he rankled her with his laid-back style, he'd been thoughtful and made her laugh more than she had in years. Laughter and anger, emotions she'd hidden beneath her stoic "nononsense" work ethic.

Her stomach growling, Kathryn eyed her wristwatch. They'd waited more than an hour for the tow truck, and now another hour had passed. She was hungry and anxious.

Lucas's duffel bag sat on the passenger floor. He'd pulled it from the pickup before the truck hoisted it off the ground. Why did he carry a bag around with him? She prayed Lucas understood her invitation. Inside her head, she heard her voice, *Lucas, you can spend the night here.* Disbelieving her own words, she cringed that she'd made the offer.

Kathryn shifted in the seat, trying to get comfortable, then gave up and opened the door. The evening air had cooled, and a chill shivered through her. Michigan weather—hot one minute, cold the next.

She stepped from the car, draped her bag over her shoulder and ambled toward Lucas.

"Much longer?" she asked.

He shrugged. "I have to wait for an estimate." He shifted closer to her. "Do you mind if I give them your telephone number? They can give me a call tomorrow."

"That's fine." She dug into her shoulder bag, pulled out a business card and handed it to him.

"Thanks," he said, palming it.

Dampness filled the air, and Kathryn crossed her arms, rubbing her warm hands against her cold flesh. Kathryn could smell the rain approaching and shivered.

"Cold?" Lucas asked.

"A little."

"Wait in the car, and I'll get this guy moving." He stepped toward the garage, then turned. "I bet you're hungry." He peered at his wristwatch. "I owe you dinner. Decide where you'd like to go." He swung around again and hurried toward the truck driver.

Kathryn stood for a moment, then did as he suggested. Inside she felt warmer, but she started the motor and turned on the heater to chase away the chill. Was it a chill or anxiety? When the heat finally came, the first spatter of rain spotted the windshield, making clean dots on the dusty glass.

Watching Lucas speak to the driver, Kathryn noticed him shift from one foot to the other before he followed the man into the building. Lucas had become a fixture in her life over the past few weeks. While she looked at him inside the garage, a feeling of comfort washed over her, a contentment that surprised her.

Kathryn's stomach rolled again. As comforting as planning dinner with an old friend, she mulled over the local restaurants. What was she longing for? What would salve her hunger? The answer hit her in the pit of her belly. She focused on the handsome man.

Despite the heater, Kathryn's limbs felt chilly. Lucas had sauntered into her lonely life, and one day he would walk out again. Could she readjust her bleak existence? Could Grandma Brighton fill her with the sense of completeness she so wanted?

Rain rolled down the dusty windshield, leaving paths heading in all directions, like a road map. Kathryn followed one droplet's journey. Like her own life. Which of the many paths would it take? Feeling foolish, she brushed tears from her eyes. Emptiness overwhelmed her.

After dinner Lucas stepped inside the farmhouse clutching his duffel bag, feeling full but uneasy. Needled by anxiety, he paused in the large foyer.

On occasion he'd had a female customer offer him an overnighter, but he'd never accepted. And at this moment, he questioned what he was doing. When she suggested he spend the night, he should have said thanks but no thanks.

In his frustration, her offer had seemed kind. But now he hesitated. Had he misread her meaning? She was attractive, single, and he had to admit the woman dragged his emotions out of hiding. And like a fool he'd kissed her...more than once. But that didn't mean he was ready for a— He halted his wayward thoughts. Why was he creating a problem that didn't exist?

Kathryn motioned him into the living room, and Lucas followed her direction, rubbing the sweat from his palms. He stood in the center of the room, searching for his sense of humor.

He was being foolish. The woman was strong-willed, practical and...beautiful. She didn't need to solicit favors from a carpenter. For all he knew she had her paws wrapped around one of those executive types at the marketing firm.

"You're quiet," Kathryn said, dropping her handbag in a chair.

He eyed her, thinking he could say the same. Instead he went for comedy. "I'm not sure what to do. I've never been to a slumber party."

She flashed him a curious look, then, to his surprise, chuckled. "Really? I notice you tote around a handy-dandy duffel bag, and I'll bet it's not filled with tools."

Her observation caught him off guard. "You never know when you'll need a change of clothes," he said.

"Then you're ready for every occasion."

"You got it." He should have told her that he'd been stranded more than once away from home in bad weather.

"At least you're a man who thinks ahead," she said, her tone double-edged.

His heart dropped a plumb line to his toes.

"Have a seat," Kathryn said, "and I'll get us something to drink." She took a step, then paused. "Cold or hot?"

"Pardon?" His pulse jogged.

"To drink," she said. "Cocoa or a soda?"

"Cocoa sounds good," he said, hoping for time to get his mind in order.

Kathryn left, and Lucas drew in a deep breath, plopping onto the sofa and lowering his duffel bag between his legs, feeling like an inexperienced kid.

In moments Kathryn returned with two steaming mugs. "Microwave. Makes it faster." She dropped a coaster on the table, then handed him one of the drinks.

"Smells good," Lucas said, amazed at the banal conversation when his mind was riddled with questions. Kathryn had dropped her "spend the night" invitation with the speed of a bullet, and he wondered if she had other overnight guests.

Uneasy, he focused on the mug, watching the steam curl from the cup and fill the air with a rich chocolate scent. He blew on the edge and took a careful sip, letting the warm sweetness linger on his tongue.

Kathryn followed his move, sending a puff of breath over the liquid. She lowered her mouth to the rim, took a dainty sip. "What's the plan now?" she asked, sliding her tongue across her upper lip and licking the froth.

Lucas's belly tightened. He swallowed hard, grasping for something to say. Plan? He had no plan "Me?"

Katherine nodded. "The mechanic said it could be a few days before the truck's ready. I wondered what you'd planned to do."

Mortified, he sat like an idiot, trying to regain his composure. "I, uh, I need to make arrangements...." He floundered.

"I was thinking if you need a car tomorrow, you could drive me to visit Grandmother, then use mine."

"Thanks, but you don't owe me—"

"I'm not doing this for you, Lucas. It's for me. I need the job finished before my grandmother's released from rehab. This is the perfect spot for her to recuperate. And the best way to get her here permanently."

"Right. Exactly." He scuffled to organize his misguided thoughts. "I'll be fine tomorrow. I can call my cousin Jon. He owns a couple of cars."

"Whatever works for you. I just want you to know that I appreciate everything."

Everything? He wound his way around that word without responding. Lucas caved into the sofa cushion wishing he'd walked home…anything, rather than try to understand a woman who sent him a curve with every sentence.

One minute she was hot; the next, cold like the weather. He found himself filling in the blanks between her words, then playing hide-and-seek with her meanings. And why? He knew, but he was unwilling to deal with it.

He noticed the time, surprised that it had crept to ten o'clock. He waited for Kathryn's next move.

Finally she rose and picked up the mugs. "I'll rinse these out and be back in a flash."

He sat, nailed to the sofa, wondering if the bedroom on this floor was hers. One day he'd borrowed a pillow to take a nap. A short snooze did wonders.

Kathryn appeared in the foyer doorway and beckoned to him to follow.

He grasped the handle of the duffel bag and shot

to his feet. She'd already started up the stairway when Lucas hit the foyer. He followed.

At the top of the stairs Kathryn made a left turn and flung open the first door, snapping on the light. "The bathroom's here," she said. "You'll find a new toothbrush in the medicine cabinet. Clean towels are on the rack."

Lucas glanced inside and nodded. Toothbrush? Did she buy them by the case? He chided himself.

Further down the hall she opened another door, turned on the overhead light and entered.

Lucas traipsed behind her, but faltered when he saw the room. Flowered wallpaper dressed the walls, and pink carpet covered the floors. The room was definitely feminine. Lucas gaped at the white spread dotted with pink rosebuds and decked with a pile of lacy pillows.

Kathryn faced him and chuckled. "Sorry. I don't have a manly bedroom for you."

Questioning why she'd want to sleep in a mannish room, Lucas shrugged and gave out a gallant chuckle. "Beggars can't be choosers." Hearing his brainless comment, he grimaced.

Avoiding her gaze, he headed across the soft carpet and discarded his duffel bag on a white rocking chair. When he spun around, the light dimmed, and his heart bounded to his throat.

Kathryn stood by the light switch. A small lamp on the nightstand sent a warm glow over the room. "Bright enough?" she asked.

"Bright enough for what?" he blurted before he calmed his addled mind.

"For whatever." She shrugged and backed out the

door. "I'll see you in the morning. If you're not up, I'll leave the coffee plugged in. I'm sure you won't be far behind." She grinned and closed the door.

Lucas stood in the center of the room, his skin as rosy as the glow from the lamp. Grateful that she hadn't seen his red face, he sank onto the bed and buried his embarrassment in his hands. Why had he imagined that Kathryn's invitation was any more than a kind offer? Now he realized she needed to apologize and this was her way.

But what about his need?

He shook his head and steered himself out to the hall and into the bathroom for a cold shower. As the brisk water sprayed over him, Lucas pondered what he would have done if Kathryn had wanted to make love. He'd been unprepared for that in every way. No. He'd have avoided it somehow.

But the possibility lingered. Too much time had passed since he'd touched a woman, felt her warm skin against his. But the choice was his. He'd had offers, but with offers came commitment. Lucas didn't want obligations to any woman. Marriage was out of the question…and what woman didn't want to be a wife and mother?

He rinsed and towel dried, then looked into the mirror and dragged his fingers across his whiskered jaw. Wondering if he'd find a razor, Lucas opened the medicine cabinet. None. He'd toss one in his duffel bag when he got home.

Lucas stepped into the hallway and leaned over the banister. The foyer was dark below except for a dim shaft of light edging across the floor. A kitchen night-light, he assumed. Kathryn was in her room.

He should have known the downstairs bedroom was hers. The room was practical. No ruffles or lace there. The regular-size bed was covered with a plain beige spread, and beneath, he recalled, the white pillowcase. Nothing fancy, not a single doily in sight.

Inside his room Lucas dropped his jeans on the floor and grinned as he crawled beneath the pink sheets. Why was this room all fluff and ruffles? He snapped off the light and stretched out, easing his tense back against the unfamiliar mattress.

In the dark he envisioned Kathryn, a floor below him, curled up in her own bed. His imagination galloped ahead of him seeing her high cheekbones pressed against the pillow, her dark shoulder-length hair splayed against the white pillowcase, her small hand tucked beneath her chin. And under the sheet? Was she wearing a filmy gown of pale-blue or maybe some of those baby-doll things he'd seen in the department store.

Chuckling, Lucas rolled over and wrapped his arms around the second pillow, drawing it against his chest. If he were a betting man, he'd wager she was bound neck high in a white flannel nightgown.

"Listen, I'd better get out of here," Jon said, pulling off his canvas gloves. "I'm not sure your special lady will like a stranger in her house."

Tensing, Lucas held up his hand and frowned. "Listen, pal, watch the 'special lady' lingo, and you're not a stranger. We're related."

"Did you ask her if your family could come calling?"

Lucas chuckled. "I hadn't considered this a 'come

calling' situation. I needed your muscle." He smacked Jon's flabby arm. "What little there is of it. You need to beef those babies up, Jon."

"Too much couch time. You're right."

"So have you used a little brain muscle? Any ideas about the situation with my father and the company?"

Jon shook his head, a guilty glint in his eyes. "I hate to meddle, Lucas, but I really haven't come up with a thing. Nothing that would satisfy everyone."

"Well, don't give up on me, okay?"

"You know I won't." Jon flexed his wrist and checked his watch again. "I should be on my way."

"No, wait. I'd like you to meet her, and no kidding, she won't mind that you're here. She'll probably give you dinner for helping."

The sound of stones crunched on the driveway, and Lucas shrugged. "Anyway, she's here. Remember, I'm just a carpenter."

In seeming defeat, Jon dropped his arms to his sides and leaned against a doorjamb.

Kathryn's heels tapped on the linoleum, and she strode to the porch, like always, to check his progress. Today, when she came through the doorway, she faltered.

"Kathryn, this is my cousin, Jon Tanner. Jon, Kathryn Palmer."

"Nice to meet you," Jon said, stretching his hand toward her. She stepped closer with a cautious smile and gave him a firm handshake.

"Jon helped me carry in some wallboard."

"I see. Well, thanks, that's very kind of you."

Lucas wondered what Jon thought of her. Today she had dressed in a light-purple suit that nestled her slender hips and showed off her curvy figure. The color—lilac, he guessed—made her eyes misty and inviting, like a hazy purple sunset.

When Lucas tuned in, he noticed Jon had scooted closer and was flashing her his boyish grin. Kathryn laughed, her voice ringing like a shop bell that tinkles when a patron opens the door.

Lucas eyed the situation and stepped past Jon to Kathryn's side. "Listen, man, I'm sorry you have to leave so soon. I know you said you were in a hurry."

Jon's jaw dropped for a fleeting moment. "Right," he said, giving Lucas a sly grin, then turned to Kathryn. "It was very nice to meet you."

Lucas grabbed his arm and ushered him through the back door, his grip tightening as they walked.

"Hey, I get the point, man. She's yours."

"Not exactly, but it's a possibility," Lucas said. "I like the woman. Anyway, you're hooking up with Colleen, last I heard."

Jon chuckled. "I guess I did say that." He clamped Lucas's shoulder. "She's a good-looking woman, pal." He gave Lucas a wink and slid into his streamlined sports car. "By the way, if you need to borrow my sedan, let me know. I drive this little number in the summer."

"Thanks, Jon." Lucas gave the window frame a thump. "I'll be in touch."

Jon nodded, then flew down the road, leaving a rooster-tail trail of dust in the air and a twinge of jealousy in Lucas's chest.

Chapter Six

Kathryn looked out the window. Lucas had been gone with her car for a couple of hours, and she wondered what was keeping him. She had no worry about her vehicle. But what was the holdup?

In fact, too many things seemed to be held up. The plumber hadn't shown as promised, and this meant no progress on the bathroom. Kathryn was disappointed. The furnace company had been delayed, too. The duct work needed to be brought in before the wallboard went up.

Patience. That's what she needed. Lucas amazed her. No matter what happened he seemed to roll with it. Knock him down and he stood up like one of those punching-bag clowns. Except Lucas was no clown. He'd become more appealing and handsome to Kathryn every day.

She remembered the first time she'd seen him touched by the spring sunshine. She remembered his muscular, bronzed arms, accented by blond hair, and his sand-colored hair streaked with platinum.

Curling her legs beneath her, Kathryn picked up her novel and flipped it open at the bookmark. She scanned the pages, struggling to recall the plot. Since she'd been visiting her grandmother daily, the novel had sat on the table, unopened.

She turned the pages, skimming the words until the plot sounded familiar. Finally she remembered where she'd left off. Resting her head against the sofa back, she let the story take her away.

The telephone's ring pulled her from the suspenseful plot. Lucas, she was sure, and wondered what was wrong. She dropped the book into her lap, grabbed the cordless phone at her side, and said, "Hello."

"Anne," Kathryn said, surprised to hear her sister's voice. "How are you?" But judging by her sister's tone, the question was moot.

"Not good, Kathryn."

Her tremor triggered Kathryn's concern. "Is it one of the kids?" Her chest constricted.

"No, they're fine. It's me...well, it's me and RTom."

"Don't say it, please. Not you two?" Though in younger years Kathryn had been jealous of Anne, today she meant what she'd said. With three children and what had always seemed a good, solid marriage, Kathryn didn't want to hear bad news.

"I haven't given up yet, but...something's not right. I feel it, and I, well, I don't know what to do." Anne's sobs echoed across the telephone line, and Kathryn ached at hearing her sister cry.

Usually Kathryn did the crying. In their school

years, Kathryn had always been the one weeping into her pillow while Anne skipped off with friends or snuggled up to some boy. Today was different.

"Are the kids there, Anne?" Kathryn asked, hoping they weren't hearing their mother's distress.

"No. I'm alone."

"What's going on?" Kathryn asked.

"Little things. Tom's staying out late. He says it's work, but things have changed. He's either very distant or overly attentive. You know, like he's covering something. We're far beyond the 'seven-year itch,' but...I'm worried it's another—" Her voice trailed off.

Kathryn nodded to herself. Not seven, but maybe the fourteen-year itch.

"Don't jump to conclusions, Anne. Have you talked with Tom?" The question sounded good, but would he be truthful? Kathryn knew about those lies from her college years. The humiliating memories shuffled through her. She wouldn't wish those feelings on an enemy.

"I've hinted that things aren't right," Anne said. "Tom says he's working too hard. I guess I haven't come right out and asked because...I'm afraid of the answer."

"Sometimes the answer's better than guessing." She'd learned that from experience, too. At least Anne would know the truth. Kathryn had walked away with her head high. No more whispers behind her back.

Kathryn pushed away the recollections. "If he's seeing someone, Anne, then you'll have a fair fight.

Right now you're fighting a shadow. Do you understand?''

Silence, then a sniffle.

''You're right,'' Anne said. ''I need to get some gumption and…I appreciate your listening, Kathryn. I couldn't call Mom and Dad. They'd have a fit.''

She'd hit that nail on the head. Their mother had placed Anne on a pedestal—the epitome of a happy marriage. Telling them would only add to Anne's grief.

''Look, Anne, call me anytime. Night or day,'' Kathryn said, wishing she'd monitor her mouth before using it. Still, this was the first time her sister was really in need, and despite the past, Kathryn longed to offer her some sage advice. ''See if Tom's folks will watch the kids for a week and you two take a vacation. You have to find that old spark you had once. Romance can fade. You need to revitalize it.''

Kathryn might have laughed if the situation wasn't so serious. Who was she to tell her ''perfectly married'' sister about romance and resparking her marriage?

''That's an idea. Maybe we could,'' Anne said, her voice not as confident as the words.

''You're welcome to come here, Anne. You and the kids.'' The words were out before she could stop herself. What would she do with three kids underfoot and a sister she'd disliked much of her youth? But hearing Anne's desperation blanketed the bad feelings.

''Thanks, Kathryn. I love you.''

Like a railroad spike, the three words nailed Kathryn's heart. "I love you, too, Anne." The alien words jolted Kathryn's inner ear.

When she set the receiver on the table, Kathryn fell back and stared at the ceiling. What had she done? Said "I love you" to her sister, which was a first. And next, she'd invited the whole pack to invade her farmhouse.

The kids. Her heart melted at the thought of the children. She hadn't seen them for nearly three years. Kimberly had been eight. She'd be eleven now. What would life be like with children all over the place? Kathryn couldn't imagine.

Hearing a rap on the door, she put her feet on the carpet, but before she stood, Lucas's voice reached her. "It's me," he said. "Sorry I'm late. I had to take care of some unexpected business."

Kathryn's ears perked up, and curiosity nipped at her. "Business?" she asked.

"Nothing dramatic," he said.

She lingered a moment, hoping to hear more.

"Your car rides like a dream," he said, dropping the "unexpected business" topic. "I ought to buy one."

Buy one? How could a carpenter afford a sports car like hers? Ludicrous. Yet a man who watched the birds and smelled the flowers might come up with a hare-brained scheme to put his savings into a sports car.

She didn't bother to respond, and he didn't wait for one. Instead he wandered across the room and took the book from her lap.

"Good story, don't you think?" he asked.

"Don't tell me the ending," Kathryn blurted out,

hoping he wasn't one of those who loved to ruin a novel.

"Can't. I'm still reading it. Looks like I'm farther than you." He flipped through the leaves and turned around a dog-eared page to show her. "I'm right here."

Kathryn felt her mouth drop open as she gaped at his place marked in *her* book. "You mean you're reading *my* novel?"

"You don't mind, do you? I don't read it when you are."

"Now, that makes sense." Her back stiffened, and she felt her shoulders draw upward like a puff adder. No wonder her bookmark was in the wrong place. "And when is it that you do this reading?"

As the question fell from her lips, she flexed her palm toward him. "Never mind. I know. During one of your breaks, no doubt."

He plopped the novel into her hands, a grin spreading across his face. "Listen, I didn't mean to rile you. I can buy my own novel." He pointed to the table. "It was lying there, and I picked it up. The thing caught my interest."

Kathryn squirmed with embarrassment. She was making a big deal over a paperback book. "Forget it. Just don't move my bookmark."

This time he did the flex-palm action. "No. No, I'll buy my own novel. Sorry about the bookmark. It fell out while I was reading."

Looking at his face and imagining hers, the situation struck her as ridiculous. Her laugh started softly, but the more she pictured them raving over a five-dollar paperback book, the more foolish she felt, and the louder she snickered.

Being stubborn, Lucas clamped his lips together, refusing to make a noise, but Kathryn watched his tight belly begin to quiver, until a loud guffaw burst from his throat.

Lucas dropped beside her on the couch, wrapping his arms around her shoulders and burying his face in her neck. Though their chuckles filled the air, a wonderful sensation filled Kathryn's heart. Laughter and Lucas were the best medicine for a lot of things.

After a full day at the firm, then a visit to her grandmother, Kathryn drove home, weary. Grandma Brighton was making good progress. In another two weeks the therapist had mentioned she'd be ready to go home…if she had a place to stay.

Kathryn couldn't fault Lucas. He'd worked hard. In fact, he'd worked longer hours than usual, while staying at the house waiting for his transmission. But things took time, and they were dependent on so many other tradespeople. The plumber had only finished the day before.

Frustration inched up Kathryn's back. Her mother had moaned that she'd have to come back to Michigan herself if Kathryn couldn't make decent arrangements. No way would she allow her mother to assume the burden. Grandma Brighton would come to the farmhouse, do or die.

Her mind sought quick answers. How could she help Lucas get the job finished? The sitting room and porch could be delayed. The bedroom and the bath were Kathryn's priorities. Did Lucas have part-time help, other carpenters who stepped in to finish a job? That cousin? She'd ask him.

Ironically, Lucas's leaving weighed on her mind like cement blocks. Her life was a paradox of wanting him to hurry while praying he'd slow down. Yet, at the moment, the situation pressed for action.

Kathryn pulled into the driveway. She'd always felt a sense of comfort seeing his pickup sitting there, but with it in the garage, she didn't breathe easily until she heard a bang or thud as she entered. Lately the noise had become soothing music to her ears.

As she opened the door, rather than the familiar sounds of construction, a succulent aroma wrapped around her senses. She followed her nose through the foyer straight into the kitchen. In the doorway she gaped at Lucas, standing in front of the stove with a dish towel tucked in his waistband and a pot holder in his hand.

"What in heaven's name are you doing?"

He swung around as if she'd hit him with a hammer. "Kat! Whoa, I didn't hear you." Shock etched his face.

She grimaced at the nickname. Between the microwave buzzer and the ting-ting of a lid rising and falling against a pan on the burner, she wasn't surprised. She put her hands on her hips. "I asked what you're doing?"

"Guess," he said, his smile lines deepening.

"Aha, I know," she said, using her most sarcastic voice. "You're remodeling my farmhouse."

His grin faded only a smidgen. "That, too…but at the moment, we're celebrating. My pickup's ready, and I'm preparing a gourmet dinner as a thank-you."

Frustration rattled in her head. "But..." She faltered. The man wouldn't understand her *but*. Instead, he smelled roses and watched cedar waxwings. Knowing her battle was hopeless, she relaxed her shoulders.

"Lucas," she said, approaching him with as much patience as she could muster, "I appreciate your thoughtfulness. I am tired—"

"And hungry?"

Controlling her frustration, she lifted her index finger and pressed it against his lips. Before she could finish her sentence, he kissed her finger, then caught it in his hand along with the pot holder.

Kathryn's knees weakened and a gentle tremor worked from her finger to her heart.

"I'll get back to work after dinner," he said. "Now, I want you to get comfortable. We'll eat in a few minutes, and you can tell me all about Ida."

Defeated, she turned and as she passed the counter, she caught a glimpse of an open cookbook. Her only gourmet cookbook—a Christmas gift from a co-worker, someone who didn't know her well at all.

When she reached the dining room, she halted. Lucas had set the table with place mats, her best china and a set of candlesticks she didn't remember owning. Not only did he use her pillow and read her novel, but the man spent time looking through her drawers and cabinets.

Instead of feeling anger, she grinned. How could she be irritated at the only person in the world—other than her mother—who cared enough to cook her a special dinner?

In her bedroom she slid out of her work clothes,

then searched her closet for something casual, and…
And what? Pretty? Feminine? Sexy? Her heart
skipped a beat even thinking the words.

Rebelling against her musings, Kathryn turned,
looking for her favorite jeans, the faded baggy ones.
But the rich, tangy scent from the kitchen followed
her like a beckoning finger, and she gazed into her
closet one more time.

Against the wall she spotted a denim dress she'd
worn only once. The stonewashed fabric was adorned
with a pretty patchwork inset on the bodice. Soft, casual, but different…like Lucas. She slipped the loose
slim-line dress over her head, the cap sleeves rounding her shoulders, then slid on a pair of denim flats.

Glancing in the mirror, she daubed on peach-
colored lipstick, then pulled the sides of her hair away
from her face and caught the strands in a clip, leaving
the rest hanging to her shoulders. She eyed herself
again. Lucas was right. She looked more relaxed.

A clang echoed down the hallway, followed by Lucas's voice. Kathryn chuckled, picturing Lucas banging a wooden spoon against a pan lid and calling,
"Come and get it." She took one deep breath and
followed the delectable aroma into the dining room.

As she approached the doorway, she faltered. Lucas had dimmed the lights and lit the candles. Inside
the room he stood beside a chair and held it, his look
caressing her as she lowered herself into the seat.

He joined her, his appreciative gaze never wavering, his eyes like a spring sky.

"You're beautiful, Kat. I like your hair that way."
He reached over and ran his fingers along the strands
to her shoulder. "It's very flattering."

She swallowed, hoping to express a calm thank-you. But her voice sounded breathless in her ears.

His fingers slid from her hair and brushed down her arm to her hand. "Hungry?"

Her senses screamed. Hungry? The ache in her belly was triggered by more than hunger. She studied his gentle face, amazed he'd spent hours in the kitchen.

She longed to cover his mouth with hers, run her fingers along his powerful neck to his broad shoulders, then touch the soft down of his chest. She kept the vision in her heart until his puzzled expression roused her.

"Is something wrong?" he asked.

"No. No, I'm very hungry," she murmured, struggling with the breathless emotion. "It smells wonderful."

"Good," he said. "I wanted to please you, Kat."

As if in a dream, Kathryn watched him spoon an array of savory treats on her plate. She lifted her fork and slivered off a piece of lemony veal covered in mushrooms and artichoke hearts. Next, she nibbled on new potatoes in butter and parsley, and a blend of vegetables glazed with dill and thyme.

She had questions to ask and business to discuss, but watching him, she pushed her worries aside and basked in self-indulgence. Kathryn gazed at him in the candlelight, admiring his strong features, which seemed so different from his gentle manner.

"Tell me about Grandma," he said, intruding on the silence.

She wished he hadn't asked, since the telling would

resurface her concerns. "Doing well, the therapist said. Better than most women her age."

Lucas chuckled. "She's not like most women of her age."

That comment was truer than Kathryn liked to recall. "She'll be released soon." She eyed him, hoping he'd relieve her worries.

"Soon?"

The single word left her wanting more. "Can you get some help, Lucas? Someone to give you a hand finishing the bedroom and bath, at least?"

"I prefer to work alone," he said avoiding her gaze.

The luscious food sat in Kathryn's stomach like a lump. "What you prefer and what's practical don't always gel."

"Maybe not to you, but it does to me." He pressed his palm against her outstretched hand. "Look, Kat, I'll work late tonight. I can stay over and get an early start in the morning."

Stay over. No, she couldn't have that. She wanted too much of him. The gentle kisses and tender caresses were leaving her yearning for more. But Kathryn knew her mind. She'd marry chaste or die chaste. It was a matter of principle. She knew she longed for more from Lucas, but what did he desire?

During college, she'd trusted Bill and had faced his betrayal. She would never allow it to happen again. If she refused to put out, she'd learned that men would go elsewhere...like Bill. If she refused to give herself to Lucas, he'd look for someone new, too, if he wasn't already involved. She had to protect herself.

Drawing in a deep breath, Kathryn focused on Lucas's expectant face, washed in the lovely candlelight.

"No, Lucas, we'll think of another way to get the job done." Yet, when she saw his wounded expression, she wanted to toss her principles out the window and let him stay forever.

Chapter Seven

Vacation days. That was the solution. By the time Kathryn pulled into her driveway, she'd made up her mind. She would take off a week or two from the firm. She was no carpenter, but she wasn't stupid. How difficult could it be to hammer a few nails?

Along with Lucas's pickup, a van emblazoned with Hansen's Furnace Installation and Repair was backed up to the rear of the house. Finally. Now Lucas could make some progress. And he could certainly use her help.

Heading down the driveway, Kathryn caught a glimpse of Lucas in the backyard. Bird-watching, she was sure. But rounding the corner, she tripped over a shovel and stumbled to an ungraceful stop.

"Sorry," Lucas called.

She closed her gaping mouth and wrestled to contain the words that almost escaped her mouth.

"Surprised?" he asked, a million-dollar smile lighting his face.

"There's no word to express it," she said, biting back the sarcasm. "Why are you planting flowers?" As if she'd been sucker punched, she gave him a dazed stare. They'd discussed more than once how she needed him to complete the work. Her arms hung at her side, limp and weak.

"Hey, Kat, my love—"

"Don't Kat, my love me," she snarled. "What about the work *inside?*"

"But imagine how nice it'll be for you and Ida to sit on the porch in the morning with your coffee and—"

"What porch? There won't be a porch or a bedroom for my grandmother if you don't—"

"Hey, I figured you'd be happy," he said, his smile fading to guilt. "Look, I couldn't work inside with all that going on." He gestured to the van. "They're in the places I need to be."

"But…" She had nowhere to go with her *but.* In this case he was right.

Swallowing her frustration, she noticed he'd used railroad ties to form a lengthy rectangular area just beyond the porch on each side of the back door. In the beds, he'd planted rosebushes and summer flowers already in bloom. Along the borders were bunches of colorful snapdragons and kitten-faced pansies.

"It's beautiful," she said, pushing her biting remarks as far away as she could from the bright splatter of summer color.

"Thanks," he said. "I'd hoped you'd like it. There's a nursery right up the road. Maybe you'd like to stop on your way home from work and pick up a few more flowers. I left room."

She opened her mouth to say she wouldn't be coming home after tomorrow. Her task would be right here, keeping an eye on him, but she thought better of it.

Instead Kathryn admired the bright spot he'd added to her yard and stared, mesmerized by a small white butterfly hovering above the blossoms. She watched it flutter from flower to flower before it flitted away. One day Lucas would flit off—to another project.

Glancing toward his pickup, she envisioned him toting the flats of blooms and the railroad ties. "Truth is, you couldn't wait to drive somewhere and put something in the truck bed."

He ran his fingers through his hair. "If I'm not careful, you'll know all my secrets."

His gaze drifted for a moment, and she sensed that his banter had triggered an unwanted memory.

Secrets? Did he have secrets? A wife he'd lied about? Children he hadn't mentioned? Why did she care?

Because she liked his down-to-earth ways. He didn't try to impress people with a degree mounted on the wall or a hundred-dollar vocabulary. He was honest and kind. Very different from her stressed co-workers.

Cringing, Kathryn faced the truth. She was one of those stressed workers: in charge, in control, on guard. She was on the lookout for any man who came too close to her or her job. If some of them had a chance, they'd loosen her rung on the ladder. Not like Lucas.

She focused on him watering the flowers with a garden hose he must have found in her weathered garage. That was another project she should ask him to tackle. And the kitchen. That definitely needed remodeling. If Lucas tackled all the projects that needed doing, she might keep him around for...forever, maybe.

Alerted by a door's slam, Kathryn watched a burly man saunter across the grass toward Lucas, hand him an invoice and head for his van.

"He's finished," Lucas said, eyeing the paper. "Cost a little more than I expected, but not bad." He folded the bill and shoved it into his back pocket.

Lucas coiled the hose and left it beneath the outside faucet. "I'll saturate this again in the morning. I planted them with root fertilizer."

"Thanks. What do I owe you?" she asked.

"Dinner."

Framed by the new flower beds, Lucas took Kathryn's breath away. The sunlight played on his hair and made deep shadows in his handsome features. "I meant for the plants and..."

"And the ties, I know. All I want is dinner."

Aching with a deep, unfamiliar yearning, Kathryn longed to throw her virtue aside and say she owed him dinner *and* breakfast. Instead, she said, "Dinner. Why not?"

When he smiled, she knew "why not." She could say he was only a carpenter, he was not her type, he was a man she didn't really know...but she wanted him more than any man she'd ever known. And wanted him for more than his impressive body. He was downright wonderful.

"Carry-out or a real home-cooked meal?" she asked.

His face tugged out her response. "Home-cooked, naturally."

He smiled. "You cook, while I inspect the duct work and organize for tomorrow." He linked his arm with hers.

Basking in the fragrance of soil, sun-baked skin and aftershave, Kathryn followed him toward the house, imagining how they looked: she in a sedate business dress and Lucas in jeans and T-shirt. They were a unique...but hopeless duo.

"Delicious." Lucas rubbed his filled belly and leaned forward, his elbow on the table.

"Thanks," she said. "I'm sorry, there's no dessert."

She stood at the sink while he studied her soft, rounded curves from behind, thinking she was all the dessert he wanted. Visions of velvety flesh, as smooth as peaches and cream, inched through his mind. Images of her flooded his mind, while he sank without a life jacket.

"I have some ice cream," Kathryn said. Unnoticed, she'd shifted to the refrigerator.

"Ice cream needs pie." His tongue felt thick, as if he'd wakened from a dream. But "pie" and his blatant visions of "peaches and cream" triggered a thought. "Hey, Miss Magic-in-the-Kitchen, how are you at crust?"

She tilted her head. "Good. Why?"

"Because I make a mean peach pie."

"Talk about magic, how do you make peach pie without peaches?"

"Easy. Trust me." He rose from the chair. "You start the crust...and I'll pick the peaches."

"I'd like to see that." She shot him a smug look.

He spun on his heel and darted through the house to the front door. He needed peaches, but, even more desperately, he needed fresh air.

Beneath the darkening sky, a breeze wrapped around him. He drew in lengthy breaths. He'd had a couple of fleeting romances in his time, but not with a woman he spent hours with...making pies and digging flower beds.

He slapped his palm against the cold metal of the pickup and rested his face against the back of his hand. He needed control. He needed...

Lucas had no idea what he needed or wanted anymore. His thoughts were tied to a white farmhouse and a business-garbed woman, who, underneath, was soft and supple.

Releasing a blast of air, he opened the truck door and pulled out a bag of peaches he'd bought at a vegetable stand on his "flower quest" earlier in the day. Flowers? What had gotten into him. No commitments. No duties. No love. That's what he'd wanted. He faltered, dragging his fingers through his hair. Yet everyone needed love.

He slammed the pickup door and shoved the bag under his arm. He'd suggested the pie, so it was too late to back out now. He would make it and then escape. Their relationship was a contracted construction job. He needed to focus.

Instead of using the front entrance, Lucas walked to the back and came in through the old porch.

As he stepped through the doorway, Kathryn

looked up. "What took you so long? Couldn't find a peach tree?"

He held out the bag, and her smile sent a lightning bolt to his knees.

"You really do have peaches." She stretched out her hand for the bag.

Lucas set the peaches in her arms, longing to be the paper sack nuzzled against her breasts.

She lifted out the peaches, admiring each while Lucas struggled to focus on the knife she'd handed him.

As he peeled away the fuzzy skin, Kathryn finished the crust. He concentrated on the fruit. When the pie was in the oven, he sat at the table as far away from her as he could get.

Kathryn readied the coffeemaker and spoke over her shoulder. "So what's your work plan for tomorrow?"

Relieved by the change of subject, he answered. "Wallboard…the bathroom first. Then, I'll have the fixtures installed."

"I'm still thinking," Kathryn said, turning around to face him, "that you could use some help."

Lucas peered at her, trying to read her face while wondering what she was concocting.

"Why? I'm fine," he said, hoping to rid her of her fears. "Now that the ductwork's in, I'll move right along. I told you I prefer to work alone." Her expression made him nervous. "What do you have in mind?"

She shrugged and turned, flipping the button on the coffeemaker.

"You must have something in mind." She always

had something in mind. That's what made him nervous. "Look, I hope you didn't hire someone to—"

"Hire? No, this is free help. I thought—"

He rose, lifting his hand like a traffic cop. "No,
please, stop thinking. Do that at Target Marketing.
When you're here, let me do the thinking. Free help
is no help. If I need a hand, I can ask Jon."

Lucas hadn't stepped on Kathryn's toes for weeks,
but looking at her now, he knew he'd done a great
job. Her fists pressed against her slender hips and she
leaned forward, her glower like a honed knife.

"You're telling me to let you do the thinking in
my home." She stepped forward without relaxing her
death stare. "Well, I beg to differ with you, Mr. Tanner. I've decided you need help, and I'm arranging
it."

"Kat, please—"

"And don't call me *Kat*."

In his mind's eye, Lucas watched her arch her back,
distend her claws and hiss her response with narrowed
blue eyes. The image rippled through him like a peb-
ble on water. He couldn't contain his laughter.

Kathryn straightened her back. "Why are you
laughing at me?"

He clasped her shoulders and drew her close. "I'm
not laughing at you. I'm laughing with you."

"But I'm not laughing," she said, tears pooling in
her eyes.

His heart twisted, and he cradled her head against
his chest, his hand soothing her back. She stiffened
against him, but as the tempting scent of peaches enveloped them, she relaxed.

Finally she lifted her flushed face. "It's me."

"Huh?"

"I'm the helper. I've decided to take vacation time to help you. How difficult can hammering a nail be?"

He opened his mouth, then closed it. Her unwelcome declaration tangled his plans. With Kathryn at his side every day, for him to stay away from her would be impossible. Yet, one thing he'd learned these past weeks—Kathryn was a determined woman. She would be his "helper" whether he liked it or not.

Chapter Eight

Monday morning, Kathryn donned her jeans and T-shirt, slipped into her sneakers and pulled her hair into a ponytail. If Lucas thought she was kidding, she wasn't. She was dressed to work.

With each day Grandma Brighton became more ornery, so Kathryn knew she was getting better. She'd begun to move around using a walker, and the therapist said she'd be on a cane in no time.

Sipping her second cup of coffee, Kathryn heard Lucas's pickup. She leaped from the chair and rinsed her mug. No dallying today. They'd have the two rooms finished in a snap. The porch could come later.

Lucas came through the door and skidded to a halt. "You weren't kidding."

She shook her head. "No more bird-watching. Today is business."

"Today is the first day of the rest of my life," he said, choosing to go for humor.

She ignored his joke. By the end of the day he'd be thanking her. "So where do we begin?"

"Why don't you have another *pot* of coffee?"

She raised an eyebrow. "I'm ready for work, boss."

"I was afraid of that."

He ducked through the doorway, and she followed, eager to learn a few things about construction. Lucas ignored her and began to lift a full sheet of wallboard. To prove her point, Kathryn grabbed an end, but it slipped from her hands, breaking one of her longest nails.

"I'll be right back," she said.

She did a speedy trim and file job, then hunted through an old box in her broom closet for work gloves. She slid on the protective canvas and rushed back to the bedroom. But she found him in the adjoining bathroom, squeezed into a corner, pressing a large piece of chalky wallboard up against the wall.

"Let me help," she said, squeezing in beside him. "I'll hold this so you have two hands to work."

"There's no room, Kat. Stay back while I tack this baby in place. You can finish it."

She looked at the gadget in his hand. The thing wasn't a hammer, that much she knew. He pressed the machine to the board and pulled the trigger.

"What is that?"

"Nail gun. I'll show you how to use it."

She'd shot handguns before…years ago. She still remembered how to hold the pistol steady and pull the trigger. "Let me try."

He lifted an eyebrow.

"Please."

Ignoring her, Lucas continued to attach the piece to the studs. When he'd reached shoulder height, he faced her. "Are you sure you can handle this thing?"

"Why not?"

The look on his face made her doubt herself, but determined, she took the gun from his hand and fingered the trigger. "Piece of cake," she said.

He looked dubious. "Let me help you one time."

Irritated, she gave in.

Lucas turned her to face the wall, then stood behind her. Her pulse kicked into high gear as he pressed his chest against her back and helped her aim the power tool.

Her hand trembled with his nearness, and she faltered. "This won't work. You're making me nervous."

He backed off and shot her another of his doubtful looks. "I'll hold it then, and you give it a try." He cringed against the wall, bracing the board. "Right here," he said, tapping his finger against the stud.

She placed the gun against the wallboard, praying she'd do it right the first time.

"Wait a minute," he said, "the thing has a little kick. Press into it, and watch what you're doing."

His constant instruction irritated Kathryn, and he was still so close he distracted her with his brisk soapy smell and the feel of his warm breath against her cheek. She tensed her arm, pressed the gun forward and closed her eyes, then pulled the trigger.

The backlash was more than she expected, and Lucas let out a "Yeow" that sent her stomach on a rampage. "What?" she screamed.

"You nearly nailed me," he said.

Dramatics, for sure. But when she looked, she gaped at Lucas's T-shirt, fastened to the wall.

"It's only your shirt," she said, trying to cover her humiliation and fear. "I missed your skin."

"Thanks. That was thoughtful."

"But look," she said, "I did a good job."

"You did," he said, laughter bubbling to the surface. "I'll give you that."

Before she could figure a way to free him, he ripped the shirt from its prison.

"Why'd you do that? You ruined it," she said, admiring his bared flesh through the tear. "Now I owe you a shirt."

"I owe you my life." He exhaled and ran his fingers through his hair. "Maybe you should stick with paint."

"No." Kathryn stomped her foot like a child. "I did very well…except for your T-shirt. Get out of my way and give me a chance."

He stepped aside, and when she looked around he'd vanished. Apparently, he'd decided to trust her, and that was important.

Amazed at Kathryn's hard work, Lucas stood in the bedroom and sized another piece of wallboard. He'd known she was determined, but her energy still impressed him. By lunchtime, the bathroom had been wallboarded, except for a couple of odd-shaped pieces. Next, he would tape the seams. They made a great team.

When Lucas finished the wallboard, Kathryn was missing. He stepped onto the porch and found her sitting on a lawn chair, sipping a cola. She put down the drink and rose as if on a pulley, no doubt afraid he'd tease her about wasting time.

"Want something?" she asked, gesturing to the soda.

"Hmm? This isn't what I call a 'break,' is it?"

"No," she said, "you don't see me bird-watching."

He chuckled and rested his hands on her shoulders, fighting the rising desire to kiss her. The day before he'd warned himself to stay away from this siren beckoning him to fall in love. But he couldn't blame her. He'd kissed her first. Now he couldn't stop.

"Why are you staring at me?" she asked.

"*Admiring* is the word."

"Okay, then, why are you…admiring me?" A pink glow crept up her neck, and she lowered her gaze.

Every ounce of caution he'd garnered shriveled like burning paper. For weeks, he'd burned with fire and the blaze wasn't fading. Against his good sense he tilted her chin and immersed himself in her ocean-blue eyes.

A glimmer of disbelief flashed on her face, then changed into seeming acceptance. In that whirlpool of blue, Lucas saw longing like his own.

The flame rose to his belly and, ignoring possible consequences, he drew in a ragged breath and lowered his lips to hers.

Her mouth tasted sweet and cool like the cola she'd been drinking. He feared she might pull away, but his worst fear was replaced by his wildest dream. She lifted her arms, knotting them around his neck, and parted her lips to his eager mouth.

His heart thundered, and lightning sizzled in his

loins. He caressed her cheek and brushed his hand along her jaw, then allowed his fingers to tangle in her upswept hair.

Straining upward, Kathryn trembled as her moan joined his.

He staggered back, ashamed of his passion but stirred by her anxious acceptance. Longing pounded through him, and if he weren't a gentleman, he'd drag her to the floor and love her as his heart and mind wanted. Instead, he cradled her face in his hands and brushed kisses across her heavy-lidded eyes.

"No, Lucas, please," she said. "We've got to stop this."

Though she spoke the words, she stood unmoved, not running from his grasp or beating at his chest.

"Why, Kat?"

"Because it's impossible, and…we've ruined a friendship."

He shook his head. "No, we've heightened a relationship."

This time she did put her hands against his chest and pushed away. "No."

Frustrated, Lucas gaped, wanting to say too much and fearing what he'd utter.

"You're working for me, Lucas. You're a carpenter, and I'm…"

"An executive?" He staggered backward, hearing his father's voice.

"Not that exactly, but this is a business relationship. And not monkey business, either," she said.

Her silly comment washed over him. If she joked, even this much, they would be okay. He had to control himself, not allow desire to destroy their begin-ning. Time would make a difference. By then he'd tell her the truth about himself.

He extended his hand. "Okay, boss lady, it's a deal."

She eyed his outstretched arm. "A deal?"

"We'll control ourselves. Both of us," he said.

She hesitated, then lifted her fingers to his. They shook, a long slow handshake that tugged at his endless desire. He'd made a promise, and he'd keep it. But how?

Katherine paced the living room, wondering what to do with herself. She'd taken the vacation time, thinking she could help Lucas, but things were out of hand. She'd accepted his kisses. Now how could she stop? Every time she gazed at his supple lips, fire smoldered deep inside her.

A relationship was impossible. She was no one-night stand...or two-month stand, for that matter. She had scruples. She'd controlled herself for years, waiting for love or...whatever was meant to be, and she'd settled into her single world.

Settled. The word struck her. She hadn't settled at all. Life had settled on her. Now she feared that she'd be like her grandmother, flitting around like an aged butterfly and flirting with men half her age.

Tears pushed at the back of her eyes, and she brushed them away with angry swipes, irritated with the unbidden emotions sweeping over her. She'd lost control.

Even at her job before her vacation, she felt edgy and raised her voice in frustration, instead of being the calm, composed woman she'd always been. The thrill she'd found in whipping through a stack of statistics and designing creative marketing schemes faded like a summer tan.

Summer tan. What would Lucas look like when the sun no longer toasted his arms? *Lucas.* Somehow every thought directed her back to the carpenter who'd walked into her life weeks earlier. Her calm, ordered life had spun out of control as if caught in a tornado's swirl.

But Kathryn's tornado was as calm and laid-back as a gentle breeze. She was the whirling dervish who was spinning out of control, not Lucas.

This morning when Lucas arrived, she'd decided to keep her distance. Not just physically, but emotionally. Since they'd painted and the plumbers had finished the bathroom, she would offer to paint the woodwork and hang the border while he finished taping the bedroom wallboard. Two different rooms. That had to be safer.

When she heard his pickup, Kathryn's heart skipped like a child jumping rope at recess. How could she contain herself when her major organs had lost control? She grinned at the silly idea.

"Are you glad to see me?" Lucas asked, surprising her by coming in through the back.

"Should I be?" she asked, revealing an outward calm.

"I see a cute little grin on your face."

"Oh, that," she said, lying through her teeth, "I was thinking of you falling off a ladder."

"Ahh, and you planned to stay by my bedside and nurse me back to health."

She shook her head. "No, I was leaving you for

the vultures and hiring someone who'd get this job finished.''

He chuckled and turned toward the kitchen.

Kathryn followed, feeling weighted down by her biting humor. When she reached the kitchen, he was pouring a cup of coffee.

Finished, he leaned against the counter. The brew sent up a misty steam in the cool morning air. Lucas clutched the mug with both hands and lifted it to his lips, his focus directed at her.

Guilt poked her conscience. ''Ignore me. We've done a great job this week.''

He only nodded and took another cautious sip.

She waited, hating his silence and feeling sorry.

''Any news on Ida?'' he asked, finally.

''The doctor said that he'd release her next week. A therapist will come twice a week.''

He raised his brows, but said nothing.

''Will we be ready?'' Kathryn asked.

''I don't see why not...if you do your part.'' A faint grin deepened the smile lines at his mouth.

''My part?''

''Keeping out of my way,'' he said. ''I can't concentrate when you're around.''

Her heart rate took off at a gallop. She wiped her damp palms on her pant legs and grasped for words. ''I can do that.''

''Good,'' he said, slipping the cup into the sink and moving past her to the porch.

Kathryn stood for a moment, reviewing what had happened. Was he teasing or not? She rinsed their cups and set them in the dishwasher. After unplugging the coffeemaker, she followed him, hoping she could calm her thoughts and her heart.

Standing near the bathroom, Lucas was prying open the semigloss, a seafoam-green that echoed the border paper. Grandma Brighton liked lilacs, and Kathryn had gone to three stores before finding what she wanted.

Lucas stirred the paint with a wooden stick, awakening the pungent odor.

"Turn the fan on," he said, dropping the stick on the can lid and walking away.

Kathryn slid the newspaper and paint can into the bathroom and snapped on the fan. If he wanted silence, she could play the game, too.

Grasping the paintbrush, she relaxed, noting they were nearly finished. The soft-green and bright-purple border and towels would brighten antique-white walls. Grandma Brighton would be happy with this.

Kathryn slid the step stool into the room, covered it with newspaper, then surveyed her task. She began with the molding above the doorway and painted without a hitch. When she dispensed with the stool, the task was easier.

From outside the bathroom door, she heard an occasional thud or clunk as Lucas moved the ladder, smoothing, then sealing the seam tape. Whether joking or serious, he'd been correct. Being apart helped Kathryn's concentration.

Admiring her handiwork, she stepped back and gave a satisfied nod. "Not bad, if I do say so myself."

"Proud of yourself?"

Kathryn jumped and swung around, her paintbrush swiping across Lucas's chest.

"You scared me," she yelped, eyeing the swath of seafoam-green against his plain white shirt.

He peered down at it. "Thanks. I needed something to brighten my day."

Without warning, his hungry gaze captured hers, and her breath caught in her chest. Lucas clutched her arms and pulled her against him, the paintbrush crushed between them.

She flung her head back and searched his face, her limbs trembling. "We have a deal," she whispered.

"I know," he said. "I'm showing my friendship."

The pitiful look on his face nudged her anxiety to laughter.

His expression softened, and a minute grin tugged at his mouth, but the yearning in his eyes reflected her own. Still, they'd made a promise, and if she were ever going to trust him, she needed time.

Kathryn looked at the paintbrush, making a sea-foam-green pattern on her once-yellow top. She pulled the brush upward, and as she did, Lucas captured her hand.

"*You* could use some 'brightening,' too," he said.

Before she understood, he'd raised her hand clutching the brush and daubed her cheek, then the end of her nose. With lightning speed, she tugged her hand free and plopped the bristles against his jaw.

Looking at his smeared face, she felt her tension fade. "You look good in green," she said, imagining how silly she must look.

"You, too."

He leaned toward her, and Kathryn held her breath. Instead of her mouth, he kept his promise and gave her an Eskimo kiss. When he pulled away, his own nose was splotched with paint.

An unexpected sense of disappointment washed over her. To hide her feeling, she swiped his nose with her finger, making a bigger smear. "Sorry," she said.

"Latex," he said and smiled.

"What?"

"The paint is latex. Washes off in the shower."

"Right," she said, as her thoughts diverted to a new vision that she could only dream about.

Chapter Nine

Wrapped in steam and urges, Lucas lathered his body, thinking of Kat on the floor below, washing away the paint and, he hoped, her tension.

Filled with desperation, he let the hot water stream over him. What could he do? He'd wrestled with his feelings long enough. He was a man. She was a woman. Friend or lover…or wife.

He'd told himself for so long that he would never marry. Even saying the word sent a tremor through his gut. Yet, he'd had second thoughts—and third and fourth. Kat was a woman to be loved.

Curiosity needled him wondering about Kathryn's relationship with her parents and sister. She didn't say much, but he sensed resentment when she spoke of them. It wasn't lack of love, but a sort of undercoating, like rustproofing on a car—something that could wear away with time, but was tough as nails until it disappeared.

In many ways Kat was as tough as nails, all scratch and hiss until she coiled against his chest and purred. The familiar yearning slithered to his belly. She was as gentle and lovely as one of those butterflies in the garden. And as jittery, he added.

Rinsing the shampoo from his hair, Lucas shook his head like a wet dog and turned off the tap. He grabbed the towel from the bar and rubbed it over his skin, then dried his head.

In the steamed mirror, he saw his blurred reflection, only the hazy shadow of his true self. Had that been his life these past years, only a blur of what was underneath? What was in his heart?

Lucas wiped the mist from the glass and peered at his face. He was his father's son, but not his father's image. Unlike James Tanner, Lucas could be a good husband…and father. But until he told Kathryn the truth, he was a lie. He could be nothing.

Dropping the towel, Lucas pulled fresh clothes from his duffel bag. Handy-dandy duffel bag, recalling Kat's taunting comment.

Once dressed, he tucked his paint-stained clothes inside the bag, and went barefoot down the stairs. He followed his nose and reached the kitchen where Kat stood, browning meat in a frying pan.

"Thanks for letting me use the shower," he said.

"You're welcome." She turned around with a smile.

She'd dressed in pale-blue shorts with a matching knit top and had caught back her wet hair in a scrunchie in the same blue. She looked as cool and tempting as a Great Lake.

"Need to find my shoes, and then I'd better get

going so you can have your dinner.'' The onions and meat yanked at his appetite. He was hungry as a bear.

"You can join me," she said, lowering her gaze. "I have plenty. I'm making plain, boring spaghetti."

The words "nothing is ever boring with you" flew into his mind, but he'd done enough damage today. She'd forgiven his hedging on the promise. Now he had to show her he meant it.

"Pasta's my favorite," he said, sliding his hands into his pockets rather than chancing what they'd do if he left them at his sides. "Can I help?"

"How are you at salad?" she asked.

"Making or eating?"

"I already know about eating. Making."

"I'm a champ," he said.

In silence they worked side by side: she boiling pasta and making sauce and he washing and tearing lettuce and slicing vegetables. Being busy was good. He needed to keep his hands and mind occupied to avoid getting himself in trouble again.

When everything was ready, she asked him to open a card table on the old porch. He imagined how nice it would be with new windows that opened with ease. Now he struggled to lift one of the painted-closed casings. With a screwdriver and extra muscle, he gave a final push and it shot upward.

The warm June breeze drifted in, carrying the scent of roses, but in moments the flowery perfume was covered by the rich aroma of garlic and onions. Kathryn dished up the pasta while he filled their bowls with salad, then delved into the meal.

When his hunger had subsided, Lucas focused on

Kat. "I'm glad you've forgiven me, because this is great spaghetti."

She half closed her eyes and shook her head. "You'd say anything for a free meal."

"No, I mean it." He put down his fork and leaned forward. "And I meant what I said. I'm really sorry. We made a deal, and I stepped over the line."

"I'm no help, Lucas. It's not you alone."

Hope filled him. "Then, if we both feel the same, what's the problem, Kat?"

He noticed her hand tremble before she dropped the fork and slid it to her lap. "I'm not looking for a fling, Lucas. I've kept myself too long for that."

Her words jolted him. He wasn't looking for a fling either, but she'd said much more in her comment. "You mean...that you've, uh, you never—"

"Right, I've never slept with a man. I suppose you find that odd."

"Never, Kat. I admire you."

"Sure. You and Mickey Mouse."

He looked at the hurt on her face, longing to know what troubled her. "Trust me, Kat, I admire you."

Her chin drooped and her words were lost.

Lucas rose and knelt at her side. "What is it? Tell me."

Tears misted along her lashes, and he had all he could do but to take her in his arms. "Look, Kat, if anyone hurt you...if—"

"Only my pride. Nothing more. It was years ago." Finally she lifted her chin and looked at him. "I'm sorry. I guess your 'trust me' took me back too far."

"But you can trust me." As he said the words, his masquerade grew in his thoughts.

"I haven't trusted anyone since college. It's too long a story, and it's not important."

"But it is important."

She slid her chair back, and Lucas rose, waiting and hoping that she'd open up. He couldn't make it better, but maybe saying the words would salve the hurt.

"Are you finished?" Kat asked.

"Sure am. It was great." He grabbed up his plate and salad bowl. "Let me help you clean up. Then, we can go outside and get some air. What do you say?"

She nodded.

Once they'd settled on the lawn chairs, Lucas folded his hands in his lap and wondered if this were the time to confess his family's identity. Maybe she would open up and tell him what bothered her. Then again, maybe it would be one more "trust" issue that would undo them forever. He'd cornered himself into a dilemma.

With the sun low in the sky, the afternoon breeze had cooled. Kat looked off in space, and Lucas kept his mouth closed, hoping she'd be bugged by the silence and finally talk to him.

"I can smell the roses," she said.

He only nodded, his own senses tangled in her nearness, longing to brush her cheek or thread his fingers through her hair.

"I dated a man for a couple of years in college. Bill Jeffers. I trusted him."

Waiting, the silence pressed against Lucas's chest.

"I suppose it's silly, but I envisioned marriage and a family with Bill. Then he changed. At first he seemed to understand my values. I'd known too many college girls who'd given themselves to one of the trust-me-I-love-you guys and then came out empty-handed and sometimes pregnant. That wasn't for me."

Lucas's back muscles tightened. He was astounded at the indignation he felt for the unknown college man who'd offended her. "He didn't get rough with you, did he?"

Kathryn shook her head. "For a long time he was tender and kind, but the more I said no, the more persistent he became. The whole thing was humiliating."

Thinking of his own uncontrolled desires, Lucas sank deeper into the chair.

"It's not that I didn't feel the same emotions. I wasn't dead," she said. "But the stakes are different for a woman. We're the ones who get pregnant."

The story was a familiar one to Lucas. He knew college men, even high school guys, who strutted around crowing about their conquests until the girl broke the bad news. Most of the *heroes* had faded into the sunset.

"So you broke it off?" Lucas asked.

"I should have," Kat said, "but I grew up in the shadow of a very attractive sister. I didn't want to feel defeated. I wanted someone…like Anne always had."

"Then, he broke up with you?"

"Not in the way you'd think." A look of pain shadowed her face, and Lucas was sorry he asked. "While I was clinging to the relationship, Bill was clinging to one of my friends. Every one knew…but me. No one said a word until I heard that Jessica was pregnant.''

Her shoulders slumped. ''I'd been a fool.'' She drew in a lengthy breath.

Giving in to his urge, Lucas brushed his fingers along her arm. ''He was the fool, Kat, not you.''

''But I believed his lies, trusted his excuses. I didn't suspect anything.''

Her words punched him in the gut. He'd done the same to her, leading her to believe he was an independent carpenter when he was really independently wealthy.

''I have a difficult time trusting now,'' she said. A nervous chuckle issued from her throat. ''Once I thought that maybe you were lying to me.''

''Me?'' Guilty, he clasped the arms of chair.

''I envisioned that maybe you were married.''

His guffaw was too loud. He prayed she didn't notice. ''Me? No. Not now. Not ever.''

''Never?'' she asked, her voice soft and curious.

''I won't say that. Not anymore.'' He slipped his hand over hers. ''Things seem different now.''

He looked at her sincere face, watching the breeze ruffle her dark hair, and longed to fall on his knees and confess his masquerade. But he couldn't just blab the truth. He needed time…time to give his admission serious thought and find the correct words. How could she trust him once he told her?

''Here we go,'' Kathryn said, closing her car door, then placing her grandmother's walker in the back seat. She grasped for courage and headed around the car.

Pulling open the driver's door, Kathryn slid into the car, ready for a barrage of comments from her unwilling passenger. She'd listened to "Why can't I go home instead" so many times, she sang the words to the tune of "Mary Had a Little Lamb."

"Kathryn," Ida said as soon as she'd slammed her door, "I don't understand why I can't go home instead of the farmhouse. I'm getting around just fine."

"You can go home when you're up to it." Kathryn closed her mouth, halting further comments.

"You have three stairs going into your house," Ida said. "I only have two."

"But Lucas is waiting there to help you," Kathryn countered, gritting her teeth. Wishing she didn't depend on him so much and wondering what she would do without him.

"You mean he's still hanging around?"

"He's working for me, Grandma. He has the porch to finish, and then he'll be gone." The words bumped against her heart.

"Finished? You mean gone?" Ida asked.

"That's right." She swallowed the vacillating emotion that tangled in her chest until she ached.

"Your sister would have had her claws in that one long ago, Kathryn. You don't want a husband, do you?"

"I'm happy being single," Kathryn muttered, knowing that her grandmother was right about Anne but wrong about her.

Ida grunted and shook her head. "You'll sit in that big house and grow old all by yourself. You won't even have a granddaughter to let you fall out the door and break a hip. At least that's a little exciting."

Kathryn bit her bottom lip to avoid the scream that sat in her throat. "It was an accident. You didn't wait. You never want help, Grandma. You're stubborn…and independent. You don't want anybody."

Ida harrumphed. "Sounds like someone else I know." After a grateful moment of silence, she laughed. "I might enjoy that hunk of a man hangin' around."

An unwelcome chuckle tumbled from Kathryn. She'd do anything rather than encourage her grandmother's antics.

"Okay, so I'm your prisoner. But the jailer has to go back to work," Ida said, pinning Kathryn with her haughty stare, "so what will you do then?"

"I have a *baby*-sitter," Kathryn said, watching her grandmother's distressed squirm.

"You what? Who'd sit with an old lady every day."

"Simon Legree," she snapped, but in truth, Lucas, in his usual kindness, had suggested he keep an eye on her grandmother while he was working. Kathryn had breathed easier and accepted.

Ida scowled. "Simon who?"

"Kidding. Your favorite 'hunk' volunteered," Kathryn said.

"Well, I'll be." She gave her response some thought. "Couldn't ask for anyone better to keep me company. And he volunteered, huh?"

Kathryn nodded, knowing in a few weeks she'd have to deal with the problem when Lucas left.

Ida leaned back finally and drifted off to sleep.

In her solitude Kathryn struggled with her grandmother's comments. References to Anne slashed at

Kathryn's self-defense. Ida was correct about Anne. She knew how to finagle attention and beguile an unsuspecting male. Kathryn had never lowered herself to those standards.

If she'd been a candle, Kathryn thought, she'd never have been able to charm a moth. Anne was pretty; Kathryn was smart. Her parents' voices rang in her ears.

So Kathryn had spent her life clinging to her virtue and fearing more rejection. She'd watched men in college and men at the firm. They were interested in lovemaking. So where did someone like her stand—especially with a handsome man like Lucas?

And what about Lucas? Had she only provided a handy pair of lips to expend his pent-up passion? Where did he go and what did he do when he said good-night? Her chest ached thinking of him with another woman. Yet, why? If she married he'd have to be an executive or someone with a good education. Laughter and good looks would wear thin. Anyway, what was Lucas's problem? Why did a hunk like him avoid matrimony? Kathryn's imagination flew.

Tired of speculation, she focused on her sleeping grandmother. Beneath all of her grandmother's barks and jibes lived a good-humored, kindly woman who, right now, probably felt frightened and abandoned. And a prisoner of her family's love.

As they pulled into the driveway, Ida lifted her head and looked at Kathryn with sleep-filled eyes. "You probably drugged my tea to get me here," she said, but her eyes glinted with humor.

"Arsenic," Kathryn agreed.

When the front door flew open, Kathryn's tension subsided, seeing Lucas in the doorway.

He bounded down the steps and pulled open the passenger door. "Now, if it isn't my favorite lady."

"You talkin' about me or my jailer?" Ida asked, tilting her head toward Kathryn.

"Do you have to ask?" Lucas said, pulling Ida's walker from the back seat. "Let's get you inside."

Ida grinned and swung her legs around, easing herself to the ground. As she clutched the walker, Lucas guided her up the stairs, bracing her as she went.

Kathryn held back, watching the two of them. When Lucas steered Ida through the doorway, he gave Kathryn a nod and smiled. He'd become her keystone—her strength and support. For so many years she'd stood on her own two firmly planted feet. Why now did she seem so incapable?

She'd changed. She remembered the day she'd arrived home to find Lucas bird-watching. Now it had become a comfortable joke. She'd caught him reading another of her novels. She'd chuckled. Where was her conviction, her time-managed life? They had vanished along with the summer kitchen. Her house hadn't been the only thing under construction.

Releasing the trunk lid, Kathryn lifted out Ida's suitcase and headed down the sidewalk, and before she reached the stairs, Lucas stood at the door and took the bag from her hands.

She followed him to the bedroom where Ida was planted in the middle of the floor, surveying the room. "Not bad," she said. "I didn't know you were partial to lilacs, Kathryn."

Refusing to bite, Kathryn smiled. "Everyone loves lilacs, Grandma."

Lucas gave Kathryn's arm a pat and made his get-away.

Making fast work of unpacking and getting Ida settled, Kathryn finished, then scurried from the room, leaving her grandmother glued to an afternoon television game show.

She found Lucas at the far end of the porch with an understanding grin and open arms. When she reached him, unable to resist, she sank against his chest, allowing herself to be swept away by his gentle chuckle and his soothing caress.

"As of Monday I'm leaving her in your hands," Kathryn said, tilting her head upward to meet his gaze.

"They're big enough for both of you," he said.

He drew her closer, and she buried her face in his shirt, savoring his manly scent and the feel of his firm body against hers while her wisdom tugged one way and her heart another. For this moment in time she didn't care whether her heart was in jeopardy, or if Lucas ever hammered another nail. All she wanted was his strong arms holding her close.

Chapter Ten

So far, so good. Kathryn pressed her shoulder against the car seat and wondered if those words would ring true once she arrived home. A week had passed since she'd brought her grandmother to the house, and so far Lucas had been a godsend. Besides keeping her grandmother out of trouble, he'd made extraordinary progress on Ida's sitting room, and now only the porch needed completion.

Though the reality gave Kathryn pleasure—no more sawdust and hammering, it filled her with confusion. Lucas would be gone. If she let her heart guide her, Kathryn knew what she desired. But her intellect kept poking her. Nothing between them was feasible.

She looked through her windshield at the head-high corn stalks rising along the roadside, the corn silk bronzed, the ears plump and ready for eating. August was a month of ripening and harvest. What month…year would she ripen and be gathered in?

She smiled. She would ripen for sure, at least age-wise. Her birthday was the following week. Would Lucas still be there? Irritation riffled down her back. Why was she falling for a carpenter? No education, seasonal work, long hours, no steady income?

Shame hit her between the eyes. Lucas was as quick and intelligent as she. And wasn't her own father a blue-collar worker? What made an executive better than a laborer? Her mother would say that she'd gotten "too big for her britches."

Pride, that was it. Her fear was other people's opinions, not her own. She'd worked so hard to show "them"—that unknown populace—that she was important…the upper crust. But what was crust without filling? And Kathryn felt empty.

In truth Lucas left her breathless. Still, he puzzled her. Little things about him didn't add up. He demonstrated social graces and polished manners that didn't fit. He was well read. He'd teased her with brief lines of poetry and used allegories and metaphors to explain things. And he told her nothing about his background or his family.

Despite her misgiving, her pulse fluttered when she pulled into the driveway. Even his old pickup aroused her emotions. One day she would come home from work and it would be gone.

When she opened the front door, her grandmother's laughter sailed into the foyer. She went directly to the kitchen and onto the porch, then stopped cold.

"What are you doing?" she asked Lucas. Her question was ridiculous since she could see they were playing a board game.

"You blind?" Ida asked.

"She's beatin' the pants off me," Lucas said.

Ida shot him a look. "Don't I wish."

"Grandma!" Kathryn yelled.

Lucas shrugged. "She gave me two choices, this or strip poker."

He gave Kathryn a wink that sent a charge sizzling to her knees.

"I appreciate your self-control," Kathryn said. But her own self-control had taken a holiday. Visions of Lucas with a losing poker hand zapped her with guilt, and heat climbed up her neck.

"Sit, Kathryn," Ida said, gesturing to a nearby chair. "We haven't been playing long. I got Park Place, but there's still some good property here. Boardwalk and Connecticut Avenue." She pointed to the cards.

"No, thanks," Kathryn said, trying to pin Lucas with an evil eye for goofing off again, but his smile dislodged her plan. "I'll get dinner."

She turned and charged back to the kitchen. Leaning against the counter, she struggled with her ambiguity. Happiness wrestled with annoyance. If Lucas slowed his pace, he'd be around longer. Could his dallying be intentional?

As she wondered, the high cupboards and old countertops caught her attention. When Lucas first met with her, he'd thought she wanted to remodel the kitchen. That wasn't a bad idea.

She envisioned her bank account flying away on the breeze. Could she afford a remodeled kitchen? Why not? If she ever sold the place, a modern kitchen would raise the market value. She would definitely give it some thought.

From the porch, Kathryn heard the dice hit the card table, then her grandmother's cackle. "Okay, Lucas. Go to jail and don't collect two hundred dollars." Lucas mumbled something she couldn't hear.

Rattled by her grandmother's mischief, Kathryn hurried upstairs and slid into comfortable clothing, pulled her hair back, then returned downstairs.

When she entered the kitchen, Lucas was leaning against the counter swigging a cola. He lowered the can and stared at her.

Kathryn paused in the doorway, admiring the sweep of his shoulders, his trim waist and full, strong legs that she could imagine wrapped around hers, his warm breath against her neck, his eyes filled with passion.

Ashamed of herself, she curbed her wild thoughts. "Game over?" she asked, keeping her voice steady.

"We quit," he said. "Glad I steered clear of poker. That woman would've had me naked as a newborn."

The image ruffled Kathryn's thoughts again. "You're a smart man."

"Smarter yet when I reminded her she was missing one of those horrible talk shows she loves."

Kathryn grinned. He knew more about Ida than she did. She opened the refrigerator and pulled out the steaks, keeping her mind tuned to dinner and not Lucas.

Yet, gratitude spurred her to face him. "I can't thank you enough for all you're doing. I'm paying you to remodel and you're…" She faltered, noticing his expression. "I was serious, and you're grinning."

"You make me smile, Kat."

He stepped toward her, and her heart rose to her

throat. She tensed, ready to drop the meat and wrap her arms around his neck.

Instead he took the steaks from her hands. "Let me help. You want me to grill these outside?"

His movement had thrown her off balance, and she chided herself for the assumption. "Good idea, if you don't mind," she said. "You do that while I make a salad and cook a veggie."

In a second he'd gathered the cooking tools and headed for the yard. Lucas hadn't touched her in days. Though it was best, she missed his gentle caress and unexpected kisses. Perhaps he was going through withdrawal, too, knowing he would be leaving.

Kathryn surveyed the kitchen and reevaluated the remodeling idea. Tonight she'd ask him for an estimate.

Lucas plucked a weed from the flower beds, admiring the profusion of blooms and drinking in the sweet scent of the roses. The warm sun spilled across his arms, and he glanced back at the house, hoping Ida was caught up in her TV game shows so he could have a breather.

Lucas was fond of the elderly woman. She was a hoot. When he reached eighty, he hoped he'd enjoy life as much as she did.

As always, Kat filled his mind. Her presence warmed him more deeply than the summer rays. He glanced down at his fading tan and headed for the canvas recliner. Lowering himself into the chair, he pulled off his shirt and stretched out.

He looked at the sky, then closed his eyes. In another couple of days the porch would be finished. He had dreaded the day, but now Kat suggested the kitchen remodeling proposal. He hadn't accepted the job yet, but he'd drawn up floor plans. Tempting himself again.

In honesty Lucas had been only partly surprised when she asked about the remodeling. Facing the job completion, the sense of loss had struck him like a sledgehammer. He'd dallied as much as he could, playing games with Ida and coming up with hokey delays to avoid the inevitable.

But his father's plight weighed on him, too. He'd talked with Jon again, hoping for a miracle. But he had none. His cousin's only suggestion was to be honest and lay it on the line with his father. Peace between Lucas and James Tanner would be lost if he did that. And he'd made the vow to his mother.

The deal he'd made with himself to finish Kat's addition and return to Tanner Construction was being thwarted by her request for a remodeled kitchen. How much longer could he delay?

Lucas lifted his eyelids and squinted at a goldfinch swooping from the thistle feeder to a nearby tree. The bird's unique flight, its undulating flutter, intrigued him. He shielded the sun above his brow and followed the bird's path.

With his apartment closer to the city, he didn't have the opportunity to loll around enjoying nature. No fragrant flower beds, no bird baths, no chattering squirrels to watch. Lucas stretched his arms above his head, wishing he could stay there forever.

"Caught you."

He twisted his neck and eyed Kat coming across the lawn. Grabbing his shirt from his lap, he sat up and pulled it over his head. But he'd noticed her voice was teasing, not like before, not her snapped, irritated remarks. She'd changed.

"Smell those roses," she said, drawing in a deep breath with closed eyes. When she opened them, she rested her cool hand on his heated skin. "Getting some sun? I noticed your tan's fading."

He swung his legs off the chair and lifted himself up. "Some woman that I'm doing work for keeps me trapped inside her house."

"And with her loony grandmother, I bet."

The look on Kat's face made him grin, the way she rolled her eyes and flashed her warm smile. Without thinking, he slid his arm around her back and walked with her toward the house.

A new fragrance followed them, not only the roses, but an exotic aroma. "You smell good."

"It's the flowers." She stopped near the beds and knelt down to admire a tight bud. "I should pick a few. They're so beautiful."

"Let me help," he said, pulling out a pocket knife. "Which ones?"

She indicated a colorful blend of buds, and Lucas bent down and cut the stems, longing to tell her she was far more lovely than a rose, but he knew she'd laugh. Instead he said something stupid. "'A rose is a rose is a rose,'" he uttered, wishing he hadn't. "Gertrude Stein."

"I know," she said, her face filled with question. "For a carpenter, you're very literary."

She'd given him an opening to confess the truth, but he backed away, offering only a hint. "College English 101," he said.

"College?" Her brows lifted. "Where did you go to college?"

He floundered. If he told her University of Michigan, she'd probe more, and he didn't want to lie. "You a detective?" he asked, hoping she'd back off.

"No, just curious."

"Curiosity killed the cat," he said, stressing her nickname. He rose and handed her the bright bouquet he'd gathered.

She laughed and buried her nose in the blossoms. "Wonderful," she said.

"Wonderful…and lucky that no bee was busy in there."

She headed off for a vase and didn't ask about his education again. He kicked himself for not using the opportunity to make his confession. But Kat's concern about trust nipped him in the ankles. Not telling her sooner had been a terrible mistake.

"When's a woman going to get some peace and quiet," Ida muttered in the kitchen doorway, balanced on her cane.

Lucas glanced at her from his ladder, struggling to hold the cabinet in place. "If you were any kind of a friend, you'd be up here helping me," he said.

"Can't understand why Kathryn buys herself this old house and then spends all her money making it new. Seems a mite foolish to me." She worked her way around the debris spread out on the floor and headed for the refrigerator.

"Be careful, Ida. If you trip over my tools, I'm just going to leave you there. Or are you hoping to break another hip so you get all this attention?"

She swatted at him from a distance. "My granddaughter's mouth is rubbing off on you, sonny. Have a little respect." But her eyes twinkled with her reprimand. "Anyway, how about gettin' down here and have some lunch,"

Lucas eyed her stepping over his electrical cords, worrying she'd break her neck. He gave up and climbed down the ladder.

Talking constantly, she made Lucas a sandwich, and he steered her out to the finished porch and the new table. Kat had purchased a glass-and-rattan model where they could sit and enjoy the yard.

After two bites the telephone rang. Rather than have Ida fall on her face, Lucas darted through the debris and answered.

With an inquisitive voice, the woman introduced herself as Kat's mother. Lucas carried the cordless phone to the porch and handed it to Ida. He tried not to listen, but he had to swallow his laughter more than once when he overheard the typical Ida-style dialogue.

When the call was completed, Ida stared at the receiver, then handed Lucas the telephone to disconnect.

"You can't expect me to figure out all these newfangled cordless things. Makes no sense to me."

"No problem," he said, pushing the button and setting the phone on the table.

She seemed thoughtful, and he wondered what Kat's mother had wanted. But it was no business of his.

Finally Ida pushed the plate away and eyed him.

"That daughter of mine. You'd think she'd be up here to see her old, dying mother—"

Lucas's sudden chortle surprised him. "You're about as dead as I am, Ida."

She gave him a harrumph and continued. "You'd think she'd leave that precious, hot-as-blazes Florida and come to see her mother, but no. Now she wants me to fly down to visit her. Says the weather is pleasant and I'd enjoy myself."

She mimicked her daughter's voice and Lucas bit his tongue not to laugh again. "You might enjoy yourself, Ida. You'd get Kathryn out of your hair."

"Now that's the truth. You know, she hasn't fooled me one bit. Lilac wallpaper! She's after me to move in with her." She shook her head.

"What's so bad about that idea? Give you both company," Lucas said, hoping to give Kat some support.

"Ah, she's lonelier than I am. What about you? Both of you dart around each other like you're doing one of those mating dances."

Ida dipped her shoulders and head around the way Lucas had seen on the nature channels. He clamped his jaw and forced himself to look as serious as he could.

"Ever seen an ostrich?" she asked. "They prance around like they're foolin' each other. Egad, they both know they're headed for the sack."

Lucas contained himself as long as possible until he was about to burst. His laugh shot out of him like Old Faithful. "Do we really look that bad?"

She shook her head. "Neither of you make any

sense. If you love the woman, open your yap and say so.''

"'Say so' about what?''

Lucas jumped, hearing Kat's voice from the doorway. He looked over his shoulder, wondering why she was home so early and how Ida would respond to her question.

Ida flailed her arms. "Stop sneakin' around and scarin' people to death, Kathryn.''

"I'm not sneaking around,'' she said, eyeballing her grandmother. "I'm home early. I took a half day.''

"Why?'' Ida asked.

She shrugged.

Then, Ida gave a hoot. "Your mother just called. Mentioned today's your birthday.''

Lucas's stomach knotted. "Why didn't you say something?'' he asked, wishing he'd known. "No one should work on her birthday.''

"I'm being silly,'' she said. "To be honest, that job has lost its spark.''

"But you haven't,'' Lucas said, grasping for ideas. He needed to do something special for her. Flowers? Candy? Dinner? He pondered the idea. Dinner wasn't a bad idea. A nice meal someplace special.

"Why'd Mom call?'' Kathryn asked.

"Too lazy to come here. She wants me to fly to Florida for a visit.''

"You've never gone there,'' Kathryn said.

"Sure did…with your grandpa. But I haven't since he died. Haven't done much of anything.'' She peered at Kathryn. "I suppose I could travel down to visit your mother once in a while, too. What do you think?''

Kathryn's face reflected her surprise. ''Sure, Grandma. I don't like you being alone. And if you moved here, you could travel without an worries.'' She twisted Ida's thoughts with relish. ''You could visit Anne and be free as a bird.''

''Except when I'm your prisoner.''

Kathryn's face fell until Ida chuckled.

''Just pokin' at you, Kathryn.'' She reached out and patted her hand. ''You're a good girl. But you need a life of your own. A husband and children. You don't need me hanging around scaring off possible admirers.'' She gave Lucas a narrow-eyed look. ''If I'm away, it might give you time to relax…and who knows.''

''Thank you for your sage advice,'' Kathryn said, embarrassed by her obvious meaning, ''but I can plan my own life.''

''Who's gonna take care of you if you don't have any grandchildren?'' Ida asked, arching a brow at Lucas.

''Let me worry about that,'' Kathryn said, her tone becoming defensive.

''All right ladies,'' Lucas said, jumping in to change the subject that was growing uncomfortable, ''here's my thought. Since it's Kat's birthday, I suggest I take the two of you out for dinner. A nice place. Any ideas?''

''Here's mine,'' Ida said. ''Since it's not my birthday, I think you and Kathryn should go. I don't want to miss TV. Wednesday's got all my favorite programs.''

"What do you say, Kat?" Lucas asked.

"She says 'yes,'" Ida blurted out.

Kathryn grinned and shook her head. "I can't fight city hall."

"Sure you could," Lucas said. "You just can't fight Ida."

Chapter Eleven

Lucas sipped his coffee and gazed at Kat in the muted light of the dining room. She was a knockout. Her hair was piled on her head, and she wore a sheer gray dress covered with soft pink and white flowers, the hemline of which rose higher on one side, exposing her long, slender leg. When she'd met him at the door earlier, he'd staggered backward at seeing her look so gorgeous.

Gazing at her in the candlelight, he longed to catch the wisp of hair that had escaped from the pins and touch the silky strand that curled against her cheek.

Over dinner they'd talked about everything from her displeasure at work to Ida's surprise vacation plans. What they hadn't talked about was their relationship.

He sensed Kat cared about him. But telling her about his wealth had him nailed in a corner. He'd been foolish to let this charade drag on so long.

Mulling it over, he found no way to tell her short of spitting it out. Yet, each time he tried, the words stuck in his throat. Talk about trust. Kathryn wasn't the only one with a "trust" issue. He didn't trust her to accept the truth. Or was it that he didn't trust that he was worth loving?

Fingers curling beneath her chin, Kat leaned on her elbow, listening to the soft lilt of a combo. As the mood struck them, couples rose, walking hand in hand to the dance floor. Lucas listened to the throaty voice of a young woman singing about longing and love, and his desire goaded him to reach out and take Kat's hand.

She rose with him, and they wandered to the dance floor, moving easily into step as if they'd spent their lives together swaying to the slow, sensual rhythm. His hand enveloped hers, holding it against his chest, and the other found the center of her back and nestled her against his frame.

The silky cloth slid beneath his hand, and he could feel the tender curve of her hip and the flex of her frame as she moved against his eager body. The inner fire he'd driven back with concentration and wisdom rekindled, and his belly ached and strained with his wanting her.

Kat's eyes were closed, and Lucas lowered his head against her hair, smelling of summer breezes and exotic fruit. When she opened her eyes and lifted her gaze to his, Lucas could no longer control himself. He nuzzled his cheek against hers and kissed the soft flesh of her neck.

She caught her breath, releasing a faint sigh, and he drew her closer, enveloped in her feel and smell.

When the music faded, they stood, unmoving, their eyes speaking words only their hearts could hear. Finally he loosened his hand, but stayed close to her until his passion subsided. If ever a woman was meant to love, Kat was the one.

"Again?" he asked.

"I think one dance is all I can handle."

What she meant was it was all *he* could handle. But he agreed, and they ambled back to the table.

Before the evening ended, Lucas insisted she celebrate her thirty-first birthday with a crème brûlée. While he sipped a second coffee, she spooned up the delicious dessert, eased it between her teeth, then drew her tongue across her lips to capture the escaping cream.

"Try some," she said, searching for a clean spoon.

"Just give me a taste from yours," he said, eager to put his lips where hers had been.

They laughed, each cleaning the spoon and basking in the warm, tender moment. When he suggested they leave, she nodded, but he sensed that, like him, she would have enjoyed sitting there for hours. No worries. No confusion. Just one happy birthday.

In the car she fell silent, and at the house he walked her inside, longing to hold her again to sway to the music that still played in his head. But as they stood in the foyer, she seemed distracted.

"Something wrong?" he asked, concerned.

She shook her head, gesturing to the small table beneath the mirror. "Grandma left a note." She picked up the scrawled message.

Lucas stood by her side, noting Ida's shaky script. "What is it?" he asked.

Kat lifted her head, tension coursing across her face. ''My sister, Anne, is arriving tomorrow with the children. I have to pick her up at the airport.''

''An unexpected visit?'' he asked, sensing more.

''She's leaving her husband.''

Lucas stood in the center of the kitchen, organizing his day. When he arrived in the morning, Kat had called in to the firm about her intended absence and was dashing around the house trying to make it ready for her guests.

Ida followed in her wake, her cane flailing in the air more than it supported her on the floor, wanting to know why Anne was leaving her husband, while Kat repeated numerous times that Ida was asking the wrong person. If the situation hadn't been stressful, Lucas would have laughed at their antics.

Now, with Kat at the airport and Ida planted in front of her morning talk shows, Lucas gaped at the mess with frustration, wondering how he'd finish the job with three kids and another raving adult in the house.

With Kat's dinnerware and pans still in boxes and only the upper cabinets in place, Lucas could imagine the chaos of entertaining four more people. Kat, who reveled in organization, had met her match.

Lucas returned to his work, knowing he had little time before the door would fly open and he'd be tripping over little pattering feet.

Bracing the final upper cabinet against his shoulder, he drove in the nail, then another, until the unit held in place. Grasping a handful of spikes, he heard Ida's cane tapping toward him from the porch. He steeled himself for one more interruption.

She stopped inside the doorway, her gaze shifting from him to the cabinets. "Can't even cook them a meal."

"She'll make the best of it," he said, grasping for something positive.

"You think so?" she asked, narrowing her eyes. "Kathryn will be fit to be tied in a day." She grinned. "Too bad I'll miss some of the commotion."

Before he could tease her about leaving for Florida, the front door banged open, exuberance filling the air. Hearing the noise, Ida headed toward the foyer.

"Grandma," voices called as she disappeared through the doorway.

Clutching his hammer, Lucas stepped down from the ladder as Kat scooted through the archway from the dining room, her face strained and her arms filled with carry-out bags. "What am I going to do?" she whispered, gesturing to the topsy-turvy kitchen. "I'd forgotten how...rambunctious kids are. And no kitchen."

A look of panic filled her face, and Lucas slid the hammer into his tool belt and hurried to her.

"You'll do fine," he said, caressing her shoulder. "This is a vacation for the kids. The weather's still warm. You can have picnics in the yard. Do carry-out like you have there. Eat off paper plates."

She looked at him with disbelief.

"If they stay out of my hair, I'll get this finished as fast as I can." A seeming impossibility, a sense of doom crept into his mind.

She peered at the fast-food bags in her arms. "Let's

eat this while it's still...lukewarm." She looked at the bare wall where her microwave had been, and tears welled on her lashes.

"Smile," Lucas said. "Keep thinking positive."

She brushed her tears with the back of her hand and sent him a pitiful grin that anchored a heavy ache in his chest. Things were a mess.

Trying to help, he grabbed a damp cloth and headed to the porch to wipe off the table. Kat followed, and within seconds he was surrounded by curious faces.

"Anne," Kat said, "this is Lucas...Tanner. He's doing the remodeling."

He smiled at Anne, extending his hand, and now understood what Kat had said the night she was so depressed. Anne was not only attractive, she was sexy.

Grasping his hand, she swayed her hip forward, making no pretense while shamelessly checking him out from head to toe. Her gaze seemed so wanton Lucas felt a blood vessel pulsing in his neck.

"These are my children," she said, gesturing. "This is Kimberly, Dawn and Tommy, Jr."

While the girls gawked, eyeing him with curiosity, the towheaded boy headed straight for Lucas's hammer.

"I'm six, and my daddy lets me pound," he said, trying to tug the tool from Lucas's belt.

Lucas grabbed the hammerhead and grinned. "Aren't you hungry? Looks like your Aunt Kat...thryn picked up some lunch."

The boy swung around, surveying the sacks of food, and Lucas patted himself on the back for know-

ing a boy's mind. Food always won out over most
things.

Kat opened the bags and spread the burgers out on
the table as Lucas stepped backward toward the
kitchen.

"Don't leave, Lucas," Kat said. "I have plenty.
Take a burger and some fries."

He grabbed a burger, then returned to his work.

From the porch he listened to the rustle of paper
and the complaints of too much mustard and no
ketchup while chomping down on the tepid sandwich.

Finished, he climbed the ladder and stood for a
moment realizing that things would be different from
now on. With Kat's predicament, he couldn't dally
any longer. He needed to finish the job and get out.

The need to "get out" fell on his chest like an
I-beam. Last night—it seemed so long ago—as they'd
danced, Lucas recognized that he had to make things
right with Kat, tell her about his father's company…his company and confess that he'd fallen in
love with her.

Certainly Kat was attracted to him. Her breathless
sighs and trembling body were evidence that he'd
aroused her passion. But passion and committed love
were a whole different ball game. He had no idea if
he was on first base or if he'd hit a foul ball.

The silence ended with the thumps and thuds of
luggage and feet bounding up the foyer staircase.
Caught in his concerns, Lucas worked until Kat's
voice drew him from his speculation.

"They're getting settled in?" he asked.

As if he'd tugged her from her thoughts, she responded, "Yes, they're unpacking. I guess it'll be all

right,'' she said talking to herself more than Lucas. ''I just hope, for Anne's sake, they reconcile.''

Lucas's stomach knotted, seeing Kat's strained face. ''Looks bad, huh?''

''It's another one of those trust factors,'' she said. ''I wonder if any man can tell the truth…be honest without omitting half the story or twisting the facts?''

Lucas turned his back and laid the hammer on the dusty table to calm himself. ''Not all men lie,'' he said, facing her again. *But he had.* He'd done exactly what she'd said: he'd left out half the story.

''And you see what I mean about Anne, don't you?''

''What?'' he asked.

''Come on, Lucas. Are you blind? She's a knock-out.''

He gritted his teeth and admitted the truth. ''She's sexy. That's what she is.''

''Did you notice how she looked at you? Eyed you up and down. That's her style. She had the guys kissing her feet and eating out of her hands. I couldn't do it.''

''You don't have to. You're different, but not less stunning, Kat. There's no competition.''

''No competition! When we were teenagers, if I even looked at a guy, Anne had a date with him on the weekend. I didn't have a chance.''

''That's because teenage boys are motivated by hormones,'' Lucas said in defense.

''And you're telling me men aren't?''

''Am I interrupting?'' Anne asked from the doorway.

''No,'' Kat lied. ''I was asking about the kitchen.''

Anne did a slow turn, taking in the mess. "We'll manage fine, Kathryn. We're all good sports." Her face filled with contempt. "Living with Tom, I had to be."

Kathryn touched her sister's shoulder. "Not now, Anne. You don't want the children to hear you." Kat guided her toward the porch. "Let me show you the yard. Lucas put in some flower beds and..." Her voice faded as they stepped outside.

With Kat's words about trust echoing in his head, his mind spun. He'd messed things up royally.

Chapter Twelve

Kathryn couldn't believe she'd asked for another week's vacation so soon. A family emergency, she'd said.

Tiptoeing to the kitchen, Kathryn hoped to have a few moments of peace before the lively brood awoke. She was enjoying the kids. She'd joined in their board games and played catch in the backyard to keep them out from under Lucas's feet. He'd worked so hard the past three days, but he had a long way to go.

She had a long way to go. Why couldn't she toss her fears aside and trust Lucas? For the first time since her college days, dreams of marriage and sharing her life with someone troubled her thoughts. Lucas was kind and affectionate…if she'd only accept his attention and trust his motives. Like a handsaw, her feelings rasped back and forth in her head until she'd become of two minds. The one, Lucas could never be part of her life; the other, she couldn't live without him.

She glanced down at her thin cotton robe and sheer nightgown, asking herself why she hadn't gotten dressed as usual. But the question was foolish. Anne was upstairs, and her presence tugged Kathryn's jealousy out of hiding. Lucas would arrive at any moment, and the old competition had marched out in full battle dress—a sheer gown.

She sensed the way Anne flitted around Lucas that she was hoping to make him a conquest, retribution for Tom's indiscretion. She could go home, then, and forgive him by tossing her own infidelity in his face.

Kathryn couldn't handle the possibility. But how could she tell Anne that she'd fallen in love with the carpenter? She'd barely faced it herself.

Most businesswomen on the prowl spent time at the bars for lunch and after work, flaunting their feminine wiles to cover the masculine cunning they used on the job. Kathryn had never felt the urge to grovel at a man's feet for a date, a quick kiss in the copy room or a hasty fondle in the elevator. She wanted more.

Yet, was she naive? Wouldn't a man like Lucas want an experienced woman, one who knew all his pleasure points? Kathryn hadn't even identified her own. All she knew was that Lucas's lips on hers sent her reeling.

If Lucas buckled under to Anne's obvious admiration, Kathryn had only herself to blame. After their kisses that had almost been her undoing, she'd put a stop to it. Excluding a gentle look or a tender caress, he'd kept his promise.

Except on her birthday.... Her thoughts drifted back to the glorious evening when Lucas held her against him on the dance floor, their bodies swaying to the music, her excitement rising until she wanted to scream in ecstasy, knowing that he felt the same.

The thought of his lips against her neck sent chills rolling in waves down her limbs. That evening, if Lucas hadn't drawn her closer and pressed her against his own rising desire, she might have crumpled at his feet.

The man was beautiful inside and out. When she'd opened the door on her birthday, he'd stood on the steps drenched in the setting sun, wearing a dark suit with a white shirt accentuating his deep tan, and a soft-gray-print tie knotted neatly beneath the collar. He'd taken her breath away.

But that was only part of his charm. He'd been wonderful to her and a trouper with Ida. Now these past days she'd watched him with the children. He was a born father. Unlike her, whose patience sometimes went into hiding, Lucas always made a positive from a negative.

Kathryn wrestled with her thoughts, then glanced down again at the silky gown beneath her robe and cringed at her feeble attempt to attract him. Anne was gorgeous. And Kathryn was trying to put a plunging neckline on her intelligence.

It was a blatant come-on. And a come-on to what? She had nothing to offer without marriage, and Lucas wasn't a man to revel in a steak's aroma without eating.

Discouraged, Kathryn put on the coffee and went to fetch the morning paper. When she opened the door, Lucas was heading up the walk.

"You're early," she said, self-consciously clutching her robe. She'd even failed at flaunting her sexuality.

He grinned. "My place is too quiet."

His focus drifted to her hand, clutching the robe, then returned to her face, and he offered her a grin that calmed her fears and warmed her heart.

"Hmm. Do I smell coffee?" he asked.

"I just put it on." She beckoned him inside, and he followed her to the back porch where she'd set up the coffeepot and toaster.

Standing beside the pine table while waiting for the last drop to drip from the basket, Kathryn caught her breath when Lucas stepped behind her. She felt the warming touch on her arms as he slid his hands upward from her elbows to her shoulders.

"You arouse me more than coffee anyday," he said, his breath caressing her neck.

Thinking of her family's presence, she spun around to caution him and found herself facing him lips to lips. His gaze drifted to her open robe and the sheer nightie beneath, then returned to her face.

Captured by his desire, Kathryn felt her heart lodge in her throat, rendering her speechless. Her hand rested against his hard chest, and she longed for the courage to push him away to show her conviction. Instead she parted her lips and covered his sweet, minty mouth with hers.

He lifted his hand and touched his palm to her cheek, and his lips moved against hers, his tongue searching and probing until a deep moan echoed from his throat.

Kathryn reeled with emotion and shame. Enveloped in the fire coursing through her, she'd not only broken their agreement, she'd been the pursuer.

Embarrassed, she turned and grabbed a mug from the table. When she faced him, he'd moved a safe distance away, but the longing in his eyes riled her senses. With trembling fingers, she handed him the mug.

"We need to talk," he said.

She nodded and gestured to the table, trying to stay calm and prepared for his reprimand. "I'm listening."

"You know what I mean." One hand slid from the mug and captured hers. "Alone. Time to really talk."

She lowered her eyelids, ashamed of her bold desire. "I have company, Lucas. Five people running around the place. There's no time to talk. We're rarely alone."

As the words left her mouth, the clomp of footsteps alerted her. She buttoned her robe at the top and stood to pour coffee for herself.

Tommy darted into the room. "Hi, Lucas. Can I help you today?"

"How about some breakfast first?" Lucas said.

Kathryn grinned at his tactic. She rose and dug through a cardboard box for the cereal and a bowl.

Lucas rose. "I'll get the milk," he said, heading for the refrigerator. In a moment he returned and set the carton on the table. "Don't forget what I said."

She could only nod. Tangled in her thoughts, she watched while Tommy ate his cereal with the speed of a forest fire, then jumped from the table and headed for the kitchen. Lucas had a friend.

Eyeing her robe, Kathryn hurried to her room to change. By the time she returned, the girls had eaten and were in front of the television, and Anne was sipping her morning coffee and gawking at Lucas.

Kathryn stopped just outside the dining room archway. How could she blame Anne for admiring Lucas? Kathryn's own desire rose, as she admired the ripple of sinew in his bare arms, the denim hugging his muscular thighs, the unruly tuft of hair above his forehead. She drew up her shoulders and stepped into the room.

"Good morning," Kathryn said, walking past Anne to the porch, where she poured another cup and settled at the table.

Anne lingered in the doorway for a moment, then walked to the screened window and gazed outside.

"This is a great place, Kathryn," she said, sipping her drink. "I thought you were crazy buying an old farmhouse, but I see the charm. It's a nice place for kids."

Kids. Kathryn shriveled with the simple word. So often lately her thoughts drifted to what-if. How would life be with a couple of kids and a loving husband? Without exception, Lucas's face appeared in her vision.

"I like it here," Kathryn said.

"You should get married, Kathryn. I know that sounds foolish coming from me, but most of the time my life's been wonderful. And then, the kids make it all worthwhile."

Kathryn eyed the doorway for nosey ears, then lifted her mug and took a long sip, searching for a response.

"Don't tell me that marriage hasn't entered your mind," Anne said.

"No, I won't tell you that, but being mugged comes to mind on occasion. It's not necessarily something I want to experience."

Anne rolled her eyes. "Come on, Kathryn. I remember you dated that guy in college. What happened?"

Kathryn steadied herself, fearing her face would reveal her feelings. "That was long ago, Anne. A college romance, nothing more."

"You dated for a couple years. That's *nothing?*"

Her sister's perception irritated Kathryn. "Plans change. We drifted apart."

Anne shrugged, then lowered her voice. "I don't know, Kathryn." She sighed and changed the subject. "You were kind to make a place for Grandma. This must have cost a pretty penny."

Kathryn shrugged. "It seems like a good idea. She needs a place, and I have the room."

Anne's expression darkened. "I can't imagine living alone all my life. If Tom and I—" Her voice caught, and she bit her lip for a moment before continuing. "If we don't work things out, I'd want to marry again." She leaned closer and whispered, "Right now I feel terribly vindictive. I'm tempted to have a fling."

"A fling?" Kathryn's stomach churned.

"Did you ever take a good look at that carpenter?" Anne grinned. "He's a hunk. How do you spend time around him without wanting to—"

"Hush," Kathryn said, worried that Lucas would overhear them. "I'm not dead, Anne, but..." She needed to discourage Anne's inquiry, not wanting her to blab romantic stories to their mother. If that happened, her mother would never get off her back. "He's good-looking, but he's a laborer...a *carpenter.*" Her voice rose, stressing the word, then lowered it again. "He's remodeling my house, not overhauling me."

"Well, I wouldn't mind a little servicing."

"Stop it! You just miss Tom," Kathryn hissed, shaking her head and regretting deeply what she'd said about Lucas. He was a carpenter, but he was *her* carpenter, the man who'd become so important in her life.

Yet, how could she say "hands off"? A shiver of longing shuddered to her belly. So often she'd dreamed that somehow Lucas was hers...to have and to hold.

"Whoa! This cabinet is heavy," Lucas said, knowing full well that Tommy had hidden inside.

A telltale giggle came from behind the closed doors, and Lucas bent down and tapped on the wood. "I think a chipmunk is hiding in this thing." He swung open the doors, and the boy tumbled out to the floor.

Lucas ached for the children. Anne and her husband's problem touched their children's lives whether they meant it to or not. Never would he put his own kids through such pain. He remembered too vividly his own.

Noticing Kathryn watching him from the archway, he shooed Tommy from the room and went back to his work. The best thing he could do now was finish the job and get out. Still, Kathryn's warm smile at his clowning with the boy nudged his growing sense of contentment.

Lucas had no idea how to deal with his situation. He'd thought he was making progress with Kat—the night of her birthday and only a couple of days ago when she looked so tempting in her sheer nightgown. He'd seen longing on her face that he knew reflected his own. But he'd been horribly wrong.

He cringed, remembering earlier when he'd overheard her talking with Anne. They'd kept their voices low, and he'd been distracted by Tommy's constant chatter, but the boy had wandered from the room, and Kathryn's voice had knifed through him. *A carpenter*. In reality that's all he was to her, a carpenter. And if that was really how she felt, she certainly didn't give a hoot for him. The reality raked through him.

And what was the point telling her about his family's business now? All his life he'd feared being loved for material things and not for himself. His father had given him objects, not love. His unhappy mother had given him as much love as she had. And in his social circle, he could never escape the stigma of having money. Only in this guise had he begun to trust. But he'd made a grave error.

Today Ida was heading for Florida, and from the bits and pieces he'd heard, Anne and the children were taking her to the airport and then going off to visit one of Anne's old friends.

The news had seemed like providence. He'd planned to talk with Kathryn alone, to sort things out. But what was the point? If he exposed that he wasn't only a carpenter, but the heir to a construction company, what would her declaration of love mean then?

The old concern that had once risen inside him like a dragon had vanished. The time spent with Kat and Ida…now, the children, offered him all the proof he needed. He could be a good husband and father if only…

Hearing her tap-tap, Lucas watched Ida amble in and brace herself against the lower cabinet framework.

"You know," she said, with an insightful air, "I have an ulterior motive for this trip."

Lucas rose from a crouched position and stood in front of her like a child who had been caught in a lie. "And I bet you're going to tell me," he said, trying to hide his sadness.

"You can bet your bippy," she said.

Unbidden, her comment yanked a laugh from Lucas.

"I know that you love Kathryn." She peered at him over the top of her glasses. "And I know something else. She feels the same." She pushed her glasses up her nose as if it were the period on the sentence.

"She told you this?" Lucas asked, his heart pinging like a nail gun.

"Doesn't have to. Any dang fool could see it if they'd open their eyes." She brushed him away again. "Now, while I'm gone…and if the rest of the crew gives you space, I want you to tell Kathryn you love her." She tugged him downward and kissed his cheek. "Now, you be a good boy and mind me."

She lifted a threatening finger, and Lucas couldn't help himself. He longed to believe she knew something he didn't. He took her in his arms and gave her a bear hug.

"What's going on?" Kathryn asked as she came through the doorway.

"He's trying to break my ribs," Ida said.

"We're saying goodbye," Lucas countered.

"You'd better hurry. It's time to leave." Kathryn beckoned Ida to follow.

Lucas stayed at his work, and when the house quieted, Kathryn returned to the kitchen, dusted off a kitchen chair, and slid into it, looking tired and discouraged. "I love being with the kids, but…"

"You don't have to explain." Amazed, Lucas realized he didn't know her at all, but he understood her mixed emotions.

Kathryn nodded. "I ache for them. And then, Anne and I try hard, but we've never been best of friends."

"But you've done what you could. And the truth is that it's up to her and her husband. You can only take care of yourself."

"Anne mentioned this morning that Tom wants the kids to go home and start school. She's torn, but I guess they're going back."

"It makes sense," Lucas said.

Kathryn nodded. "And it's convenient. Tom's company just flew him and a group from the firm into Oakland County International for some meetings in Troy. He's made arrangements for the kids to fly back with him. I'll miss them…in a way."

Kathryn closed her eyes and leaned her head back, drawing in a deep breath. "Listen to the silence. I suppose I'd better get used to it…again."

Thinking of his unwanted loneliness, Lucas's ache deepened. He would miss Kat horribly.

She opened her eyes and turned to him. "Having them here has made me realize that a solo life doesn't do much for posterity."

"You have that right," he said, letting his rancor escape.

Kathryn seemed not to notice the bitterness in his voice. "Do you have a minute?"

His heart kicked him in the ribs. He only nodded.

She rose. "Let's get some air. We can smell the flowers." She grinned. "Bet you never thought you'd hear me say that."

Her humor was lost in his gloom. Amazed that she wanted to talk, Lucas watched her head toward the door. Resentment shot through him. Why now? Now, when his hopes had taken a nose dive with her cutting comment?

Resigned, Lucas took off his tool belt, draped it over a chair and followed her down the steps.

The scent of roses bathed Lucas in nostalgia and captured his senses. Blocking out the rest of the world, he listened to the drone of a bee hovering inside a flower before it darted to the next blossom.

Watching the insect, he felt his heart stumble over a new awareness. People spent too much time worrying about what-ifs and too little time enjoying the here and now. It was his problem and Kathryn's. No matter what might happen between them, he knew he'd learned something important. What-ifs only dampen today's happiness.

Kathryn headed for the lawn chairs and slid into a

seat, resting her elbows on the arms, splaying her legs in front of her.

Lucas followed, looking up toward the August sun hiding behind a passing cloud. "Waxing poetic," Lucas said, sharing his thought, "we often do that." He pointed to the drab sky. "We've spent years looking at the sunshine and asking what if there are clouds tomorrow. Then, when we see clouds, we forget that the sun is only behind it for a little while. We fight life, Kathryn."

For a moment she was silent, staring into the heavens. "I've had a chip on my shoulder much of my life, I suppose. Since I latched on to the idea that I was smart and not attractive like Anne, I've spent my life proving I was right."

"But you are attra—"

"Let me finish. Especially after my experience with Bill, any man who gave me a compliment or wanted to get closer, I saw as the enemy. Even you," she said. "Remember how unpleasant I was when we met?"

"Yes. Among other things you've reminded me more than once I'm only a carpenter," he said.

Her face filled with sadness. "I know, and I'm sorry about that. That's part of my self-defense, Lucas. Before I'm rejected, I reject. Do you understand?"

He struggled with her explanation. Her earlier comment seemed belittling, not defensive. But maybe he did understand. Hadn't he spent his life avoiding romance to escape more rejection like the kind he'd felt as a child? He'd dragged that baggage with him into adulthood as if it were a trophy.

"I suppose, at times, I've done the same," Lucas said, wondering why he was telling her this. "I believed I'd never marry. My mother's life was miserable. I thought all marriages were like hers, and I feared being like my father, so I rejected him and all he stood for."

"I always wondered why you never mentioned your family," she said.

Her face expressed more than Lucas understood, but the look pushed him forward. "But I'm not my executive father. And I'm not Bill Whositz."

She flashed a faint grin. "Jeffers."

He took a deep breath. "I'm not Jeffers who wanted you to be something you aren't. I'm me." He poked himself in the chest.

"Oh, Lucas," she said, touching his hand, "I never thought of you as—"

"I'm Lucas Tanner…a man who chooses to be a carpenter, despite pressure from everyone."

"What do you mean, Lucas? I don't under—"

"I shouldn't be here wasting time." He rose. "The job should be finished in a couple more days."

"But—"

Lucas couldn't listen. In that instant he realized he had no hope of ever being loved by Kathryn. The reality sickened him. Looking for the bright side—he would never have to admit his masquerade.

"You didn't ask me out to dinner for fun, Lucas. And you know how I figured that out?" Jon asked.

Lucas swallowed a forkful of steak. "No."

"Because you're not fun. You're too quiet and

thoughtful. So lay it on the table, okay? Is this about your dad?''

''No,'' Lucas said, washing his beef down with a swig of ale. ''I talked to my father a while ago when my truck was being repaired. And you're right, Jon, he looks tired. I told him to give me a couple of months. That was three weeks ago.'' Tension knotted in his shoulders.

''So, the time is getting closer...and no solution.''

''Right. No miracles. No answers. Nothing.''

''Sorry, I—''

''Jon.''

His cousin paused in midsentence.

Lucas flashed a sad grin. ''It's about Kathryn.''

Jon's brows lifted. ''Okay, I'm listening.''

Rarely in Lucas's life did he count on someone else to listen to his woes. But today he laid the facts on the table and hoped Jon would have a spoonful of wisdom.

''You mean,'' Jon said, nearly rising from the cushion, ''that you haven't told this woman yet.''

''No, but I was about to, and then I heard what she said. I'm only a *carpenter*. It was her tone of voice. She's an executive. I'm nobody. It's simple.''

''If all you've told me is true, Lucas, then you've missed a major point.'' With the look of a man who had the answer, Jon ran his finger around the rim of his wineglass and shook his head.

''What major point?'' Lucas wanted to put a bag over his smug expression.

''The sister. The competition.''

''You mean Anne?''

Jon nodded. ''Did you stop to think that Kathryn

might have been concerned about how Anne would use the information?''

Lucas shook his head. "I still don't get it."

"Didn't Kat say that if she liked someone her sister had a date with him the next weekend?"

Lucas nodded.

"She was afraid Anne wanted to show her one more time which sister could get the man. Doesn't that make sense? I think Kathryn's comment was her self-defense. Her armor."

Lucas fell back against the bench. Why hadn't he thought of that? His mind flew back to Kathryn's behavior, her face, her confused look at his hasty departure. Maybe her words to Anne were exactly that, a cover-up. Could it be? Did she love him after all?

Chapter Thirteen

Kathryn slammed the car door and dashed up the steps. First she would let Anne know the children got off safely, then she'd face Lucas. She tensed with fear and embarrassment, afraid her suspicion was correct.

Racing up the foyer stairway, she opened Anne's bedroom door.

"What is it?" Anne asked, rolling over in bed, her cheeks flushed with fever. "What happened?"

"Nothing with the kids. Tom was at the airport, and I turned them over to him without a hitch."

Anne coughed and inched upward on an elbow. "But you look like you've seen a ghost."

"No, I'm…maybe I'm coming down with whatever you have. I'm okay."

Anne fell back against the pillow. "Sorry that you had to—"

"It was no problem, Anne. Promise. The kids seemed happy to see their dad, but I know they hated to leave you."

"I need to think," Anne said. "Tom's made so many promises, but can I trust him?"

Kathryn wanted to say no, but wisdom held her tongue. "He made a mistake, Anne. You need to decide how you can live with it. It's divorce or forgiveness."

"I know," Anne said, pulling the sheet over her head.

Kathryn left and closed the door, then stood for a moment, wondering how to begin with Lucas. Confusion rattled her. Maybe she was foolish. Perhaps the whole thing was a coincidence. She drew in a lengthy breath, then headed down the stairs.

She found Lucas on the floor, his head beneath the new sink. Her footsteps roused him when she entered, and he lifted his head. "Something's wrong?" he asked.

"I hope not," she said.

"What is it? Nothing wrong with the kids." He pulled himself up, dusted off the seat of his pants and studied her.

"The kids are fine." Her heart tripped as she pulled the question from her weighted thoughts. "When I drove down Highland to the airport, I noticed..." She hesitated, seeing his face pale. "I noticed a large construction company called Tanner." She didn't have to ask. The answer was on his face.

"Look, Kat," he said, stepping toward her.

She held up her hand. "*Look*...nothing. I don't want to hear excuses. I'm embarrassed and shocked at your charade."

"It's not a charade...exactly. There's a reason why I don't advertise who I am."

"Lucas, you might have a reason, but right now I don't want to hear it. What about that old truck of yours?" She cringed at his deceit.

"I like that old pickup. It was my first. I never told you I was poor, Kat. Never."

"No," she said her voice rising, "but you let me strut around calling you a carpenter and wondering why you seemed so well-educated and polished."

"You're the one who reminded me of my lowly status. The problem's yours, Kat. I never lied—"

"Well, now the problem's yours. I don't want to hear it." She swung around, eyeing the incomplete kitchen. "How much more work do you have here?"

"I'm ready to caulk the countertops, then finish the plumbing and the floor…and paint."

His expression tore at her heart, but his deceit kept her firm. "I can't think about this now. Just get the job finished, please." Kathryn turned on her heel and fled from the room, not wanting him to see her cry.

Kathryn trudged into the house, exhausted. She was sure she was coming down with the flu, and she'd missed too much work already. But being home was difficult. Lucas was there, wanting to talk with her, and it broke her heart.

She longed to hear his explanation, but nothing that she devised made her feel any better. He'd disappointed her more deeply than he could understand, because finally she'd trusted someone.

Heading toward her bedroom, Kathryn faltered when she saw Lucas standing in the dining room archway. She looked at his sad, apprehensive face and wanted to go to him, but pride and disillusionment wouldn't let her.

"Kathryn," he said.

She faltered hearing him call her by something other than the familiar "Kat." "Yes," she said, and stopped.

"We need to talk about the kitchen."

"I'm not feeling well. Does it have to be now?"

He shrugged. "I'm at a point where I need decisions."

"All right," she said. "Let me change my clothes."

Lucas retreated to the kitchen, and Kathryn dragged herself to the bedroom, confused and weary. He needed final decisions, which meant he was nearing the end. Her heart was heavy, recalling not long ago she'd begun to dream of a future. The kitchen. A new garage. She'd grasped at anything to keep him there. Foolish.

Slipping out of her work clothes, Kathryn found a top and grabbed her jeans from a hook in her closet. She didn't care what she looked like anymore. She was miserable at home and at work—a career she'd thought she would enjoy forever.

When she returned to the kitchen, Lucas was standing on the porch, staring into the yard. Kathryn grabbed a soda from the refrigerator, then turned to admire the lovely cabinets and work that Lucas had completed. She calmed her thumping heart and headed to the porch.

Lucas spun around, his face filled with apprehension and longing. He tilted a soda can and took a lengthy drink. "Should we sit?" he asked when he finished.

She sank into a chair and motioned for him to sit. "What decisions do you need?" she asked. Her heart had made decisions that now lay like unwanted sawdust.

"The floor," he said, staring at his shoes. "Do you want the planks sanded and finished or a floor covering? And do you want me to paint the walls? I have some color samples," he said, pulling narrow strips of cardboard from his shirt pocket. "I wasn't sure what you wanted so I did my best." He reached over and handed her the cards showing varying shades of beige she'd mentioned.

Kathryn couldn't think. She stared at the colors blurred by the moisture brimming on her lashes. The tears were a mixture of sorrows: her sister's plight, the children's departure, her aching head and the loss of her friend. She didn't want Lucas to see her cry.

At this moment painting and flooring meant nothing. Only her deepest concern motivated her. "Why, Lucas? Why did you deceive me?"

His head bolted upward and she saw a deeper sadness loom on his face. "It wasn't deceit, Kat. It was survival. Do you have time to listen?"

She nodded. Time was the least of her concerns.

"Look, Kat, when I first met you, I treated you like all my customers. I wanted to disassociate myself from my father and his company. I wanted to be independent. If I said I was the son of James Tanner, I'd have pressures and expectations on me because of the Tanner name."

Kathryn listened while the story poured from his

heart: his pain as a child, his resentment as an adult, his parents' unhappy marriage, his father's manipulation and his mother's plea for reconciliation between Lucas and his father. Lucas's openness touched her, and she swallowed her hurt and shame, trying to trust him.

"Can you understand?" Lucas asked. "It's been so important to me to separate myself from Tanner Construction, to stand on my own feet, to avoid job bids because I'm James Tanner's son."

Kathryn's clasped hands fidgeted. She wanted so badly to touch his disheartened face and smooth the wrinkles from his brow. Days had passed since his deep smile lines had sent her heart on a merry chase to her toes and back. She longed to forgive him, but fear of trusting him only to be hurt again hindered her.

Finally she nodded. "I understand, Lucas, but you waited too long to tell me."

His eyes searched hers. "I know. I'd dug myself into a hole and had no way to get out. You talked 'trust' to me so long, I was stymied."

"I did," she said, realizing that the word *trust* clung to her thoughts like a barnacle.

"And then things got worse when I overheard you tell Anne I was only a—"

"A carpenter," she whispered. "I'm so sorry, Lucas. I was ashamed the moment I said the words. I didn't want Anne to know…how much you mean to me."

His face brightened, and he covered her hand with his. "I figured that out…after I talked with Jon."

Struck by an idea, Kathryn straightened her back. "Your father admires Jon?"

"As if he were his own son. He's probably wished more than once that Jon was his."

Kathryn leaned forward. "What about Jon?"

"Like I said, my dad—"

"No," she said. "I mean has Jon ever thought about going into the business? He has the Tanner name."

Lucas's jaw sagged. "We've never discussed it. Jon has an excellent job. I don't know—"

Kathryn touched his hand. "But this is a partnership. He couldn't turn down a partnership."

Lucas sat unmoving, then lifted his head, a look of hope spreading across his face. "You might have something. It's a real possibility." His eyes softened, and he brushed his hand along her arm. "Let's not talk about me. Let's talk about us. I keep hearing what you said a few seconds ago...that I mean something to you."

His smile touched her heart. "You do, Lucas. You've not only remodeled my house, you've remodeled me. I'll never be the same."

"I hope that's good," he said, tilting her chin and searching her face.

Tears pooled in her eyes. What good was anger and hurt? Lucas was correct. The here and now is what counted. What would happen between them? They had a long way to go, but today Lucas's words gave her hope.

Moved by desire, she offered her lips, and he accepted, capturing her mouth with tender abandon.

* * *

September had arrived, bringing with it warm days, and Lucas rolled his shirtsleeves and carried the paint cans from his truck into the kitchen. Since he'd patched and primed the walls in the morning, they were ready for the next coat, a warm beige.

As he pried open the gallon can lid, Anne's shriek startled him. Lucas dropped the screwdriver and ran to the foyer staircase. "Anne?" he called.

"Lucas, come up. Please."

He took the steps two at a time and darted down the hallway. He found her in the frilly bedroom, standing on the bed, the mattress dipping beneath her feet as she jiggled.

"A mouse," she said, pointing to the dresser. "Close the door so he doesn't get out."

Lucas slammed the bedroom door, but knew a determined mouse could squeeze through a minute opening if need be. He grabbed her loafer from the floor and sneaked around, shifting furniture while Anne howled instructions from her undulating pedestal.

Finally, he collapsed in a chair and shook his head. "Either it's your imagination or it's gone," he said.

She tumbled to the bed and sat Indian-fashion. "Or it's hiding. I'm not moving until we know for sure."

"We could be here for days."

She grinned. "I know. That's not so bad, is it?"

Lucas wet his lips, trying to find the right words to explain.

She inched closer. "I'm lonely, Lucas. My kids are home. I'm here." She ran her fingers through her long hair. "No one to love me." Her seductive eyes raked over him. "I'm not a bad-looking woman, am I?"

"You're an attractive woman, Anne. You know that. But I'm not the man you want."

Her beguiling smile vanished.

"You have a husband in Ohio waiting for you—a man who made a terrible mistake, but you'll never solve your problems sitting here...or making the same mistake he did. You need to go home."

Her gaze caught his, an awful awareness growing on her face. "I, uh..."

"Don't say anything, Anne. You don't want me. Maybe to get even, but you don't want to do that. You'd never live with yourself."

"I wouldn't," she agreed, "but I'm so hurt, and my life's been so violated."

Weeping, Anne told her story, and Lucas listened, offering a comment or a bit of wisdom about commitment and forgiveness...and about children.

Anne used her sleeve to wipe away her tears. "I do need to go home."

"I'd get on the first available plane. Your kids need you. And so does Tom. At least, Anne, you can say you tried."

"I need to call Tom," she said, inching her bare feet to the floor. "Do you think it's safe?" Her eyes searched for the mouse.

He chuckled. "I think we're the only ones here, Anne." He rose and stepped toward the door.

She slid from the bed and caught his arm. "Thanks."

"I never turn down a woman in need," he said, grasping the doorknob and pulling it open with a smile.

"You've been wonderful, Lucas."

"You're not so bad yourself," Lucas said.

She rose on tiptoe and kissed his cheek.

Lucas faced the doorway and froze. Kathryn's startled face gaped at him, before she turned and ran down the stairs.

He slammed the door and raced after her. "Kathryn, please, you don't understand."

"I don't understand?" she cried, turning her back on him and charging toward the kitchen.

He followed on her heels.

"I always seem to have that problem, don't I? I don't understand much of anything." She turned on him, her cheeks mottled, her eyes like fire. "Take your stuff and get out of here. I'll send you a check for what I owe you."

"Kathryn, no. Please. If you think something went on upstairs, ask Anne."

"Right! She can tell me how *wonderful* you are."

Fire raged through him, anger and disillusionment distorted his wisdom. "Kathryn, if you ask me to leave this time without giving me a fair hearing, I'm finished. I can't handle your distrust. Don't do this."

She spun on her heel, and the slam of her bedroom door was the last he heard.

Chapter Fourteen

Kathryn wrapped her arms around herself, holding back the strange, chilly breeze that swept over her. The darkening sky sizzled with eerie static. Oppressed by foreboding, she shivered in the cooling wind.

She bent down and smelled the late-summer rose, now fading on the vine. As she touched the velvety petal, the nostalgic aroma drifted upward. Kathryn stepped back, not having the heart to pluck it from its stem.

Lucas had sent her a bouquet of roses a week after he'd walked away. The note thanked her for helping solve his problem and direct his life. What was he doing now?

Loneliness had been her houseguest. The solitude enveloped her like a cocoon. She was alone. Anne had returned to Ohio, Grandma Brighton was still in Florida, Anne's children were filling their own home with wonderful noise. And Lucas…?

Tears filled Kathryn's eyes. Nearly a month had passed since she'd slammed the door on him. After he left, Anne had bounded from her room laughing about the mouse scare and bursting with plans. She told Kathryn how terrific Lucas had been, how he'd given her courage and convinced her to go back home and make her marriage work. Then she'd called Tom and the children, making arrangements to return home the next day.

Ashamed and distraught, Kathryn recoiled with the memory. She'd sent Lucas away, condemning him without listening. He'd warned her, but she hadn't believed him.

Hearing a sound, Kathryn listened. The telephone. She charged into the house, her heart pounding as it did now whenever she heard its ring. But when her mother's voice greeted her, she slumped into a chair.

"No, I'm fine, Mom," Kathryn said, hiding the truth from her mother's perceptive ears.

"I have some news." Her mother's voice gave a cheerful lift.

"About Anne?"

"No. Well, yes," her mother said, "I heard from her, too. Tom's agreed to counseling. He begged her to stick by him, and I think she will. Anne's hopeful."

"That's terrific. I'm glad." For once in her life, Kathryn meant it. "So what's the other news?"

"It looks like Grandma may move to Florida. She's having so much fun. Our senior citizen complex has Bingo and buffets. Grandma's the life of the party. She even has Ben Sloan fawning over her. He's eighty-seven. She loves it."

"That's great, Mom," Kathryn said, trying hard to make her voice fit her words.

"So don't worry. I'm letting Grandma decide, but we'll probably need more of her things sent."

Kathryn eyed the lonely room. "Glad to," she said.

When Kathryn disconnected, she clung to the receiver before returning it to the cradle. What had she done? Lucas loved her, and she'd stormed off without listening. Where were all those brains her parents said she had?

The best thing out of the whole mess was Anne's visit. After the fiasco with Lucas, for the first time in her life, she felt no jealousy for Anne. Kathryn had finally realized who she was and the real meaning of happiness—trusting, loving and being loved in return.

Pushing herself up from the chair, she wandered into the kitchen as a crack of lightning zigzagged across the sky, followed by a resounding boom. In seconds a siren's wail pierced the air, sending Kathryn's pulse on a gallop. Tornado.

She darted into the living room and snapped on the television. The white band of weather service information streamed along the bottom of her screen. "Tornadoes sighted in Oakland County heading northeast." It was heading her way.

Dashing through the house, she grabbed her portable radio, a flashlight, matches for the oil lamp in the basement and finally a pillow. Her sleeping bag was stored below. She was taking no chances.

Despite the torrential rain, she opened the windows, hearing it was a safeguard against implosion. Then, with a final look, she hurried down the stairs to wait.

* * *

Lucas climbed into his new SUV and checked his clipboard. Things were running smoothly on the job site. Life had made an interesting turn, with Jon in the office and him as the site director. The solution had been perfect, and he gave the credit to Kat.

Her name knifed him with memories. He'd sent her thank-you flowers...roses, hoping she'd rescind her angry words and phone him. He'd picked up the telephone many times, but dropped it, remembering her enraged face and untrusting eyes.

After he'd left her house he reviewed the bedroom scene and, recalling pieces of dialogue, understood how she might have misconstrued the situation if she'd been standing outside the door. Worse, a closed door until the kiss.

Sorrow engulfed him. He looked upward at the sky billowing with thunderheads. An ominous rumble rolled out of the southwest, and he started the motor and hit the radio buttons, searching for lively music, anything to drown out his frustration and the coming storm.

Instead of music, the news of sighted tornadoes jarred him. Tornadoes heading northeast toward Metamora. He shifted into Reverse and tore out of the job site toward the highway. Whether she welcomed him or not, Lucas headed toward Kathryn's. Her farmhouse stood alone on a stretch of open land with only a smattering of trees. She was a perfect target for a tornado.

By the time Lucas saw the house muted in the distance, the rain had changed to hail, peppering his vehicle. Trees bent low, forced down by the powerful wind. He skidded into the driveway, then bounded up the three steps and hammered on the door. As he waited, the rain and hail stopped, and the sky hovered with a thick, yellow stillness. He searched the sky.

Pounding again, Lucas called Kathryn's name. No answer. But her car was in the driveway, and he noticed the open windows. He tried the door. It opened. Lucas darted inside, his wet clothes dripping on the carpet.

"Kathryn," he bellowed, hurrying through the rooms, but finding only silence. *The fruit cellar.* He headed for the pantry and bent down, yanking on the trap door. When he peered down the steps, Kat stood at the bottom.

When she saw him, her frightened face filled with relief, and, repeating his name, she bounded up the stairs as he rushed to her side and cushioned her in his arms.

Drawing her trembling frame against his chest, he kissed her forehead and hair, then steered her down the steps to the concrete floor.

A static-filled radio droned the weather bulletin, and he grinned at the nest she'd created away from windows—a sleeping bag, pillow, flashlight and the soft glow of an oil lamp.

"Thank you," she said, trembling. "I've been scared to death."

He snuggled beside her. "I've missed you, Kat. Life isn't the same without you."

"It's been terrible." She searched his face. "I'm so sorry. Oh, Lucas, and thank you for the lovely flowers."

"You're welcome." Hearing her thoughtfulness at

such a dreadful time amazed him. "You know, I love you, Kat." Lucas tilted her chin upward. "Say you love me, and I'll send you more bouquets than you've ever dreamed of."

Tears pooled in her eyes. "I do, Lucas. You'll have to 'trust' me on this," she said, her voice quaking with tears and laughter. "I love you so much."

She offered her lips, parted and eager. Lucas accepted the gift, covering her mouth with his, probing, savoring the soft yielding flesh, moving against her with the rhythm of his heart.

When they drew a part, he stripped off his wet shirt, then eased Kat down and sat beside her on the sleeping bag, his arm around her shoulder, her head cradled against his naked chest. The softness of her silky hair rekindled the flame inside him, but he harnessed his emotion, more content to hold her close.

The wind howled outside while the house rattled and fretted. They clung together, sharing their past days—their loneliness and their dreams. He told her about his new on-site inspector job and Jon's acceptance of the desk position that James Tanner had agreed to without a qualm.

Kathryn related her news about Anne and Grandma Brighton, and when they feared the house might be carried away, a sudden, foreboding calm hung above them.

Then the tornado siren split the silence. Lucas drew Kathryn down against the basement wall and lay beside her, protecting her with his body. They shared her pillow and locked in each other arms, they heard the fierce rampage tearing the skies above them.

Kathryn felt the cold concrete wall against her

back, but her palm rested against the warm, comforting protection of Lucas's powerful chest, safe and secure. She closed her eyes, reveling in the precious yet dreadful moment.

As time passed Kathryn heard Lucas's even breathing. With gentle strokes, she explored the soft down of his chest and caressed his tight, corded muscles, finally allowing herself to drift to sleep.

She woke to a heavy calm, and when she turned over, Lucas shifted, nuzzling her neck with kisses, then lifted himself on an elbow.

"Did you sleep?" he asked.

She nodded. "I just woke. What time is it?"

He shifted his wrist to the oil lamp. "Six."

"Six. It's morning," she said.

He swung his legs around and sat up, giving her a hand. "You still have a house over your head."

"But the roof is still a question," she countered, trying to keep her voice steady.

He nodded. "We'll look."

He rose, hoisted her upward and slipped on his shirt. Grabbing the flashlight, he went ahead, climbing the stairs and pushing open the trap door. "So far so good," he said.

Kathryn climbed the stairs after him. The house was still standing, and her spirits lifted. But outside the windows she could see the devastation they had been spared.

Lucas opened the back door, and Kathryn followed. The yard was littered with debris and uprooted trees. Kathryn stared at a bare concrete slab where her garage had been.

As she gaped at the empty space, laughter rose in

her chest. "I'd thought about asking you to build a new garage…to keep you around longer."

"You got your wish," he said, slipping his arm around her waist. As they rounded the corner of the house, Lucas came to a dead stop. "No," he groaned.

Kathryn affirmed what triggered his lament. A lovely new sports utility vehicle lay upside down in the road while her car remained upright in the driveway.

"That SUV was yours?" she asked.

"I knew I had good reason to love that old pickup."

The morning sun slid from behind a cloud, and the scent of wet soil and moldering leaves filled the air.

"It's a new day," Lucas said, "and a new life for us. It's worth the loss of one SUV."

"I hope you always say that," Kathryn teased.

As the words left her mouth, a thought struck her, and she pulled away from Lucas's arm and ran to the back of the house.

"Kat," he called. "What's wrong?"

She heard him behind her, but she didn't stop until she reached the flower beds. Washed in sunlight, the single white rose stood tall, glistening with the dewy rain. She used her fingernail to break the stem, then lifted the fading blossom, clutching it to her chest and drawing in the sweet fragrance.

Lucas watched her in silence, a quizzical expression on his face. "What are you doing?"

"You told me to take time to smell the roses," she said. "I am."

The lines in his handsome face crinkled, and Lucas gave her the most beautiful smile she'd ever seen.

Epilogue

"Mommy read?" Jimmy asked, poking his favorite book at his mother.

"One minute, sweetie. Mommy's reading Grandma's letter."

Kathryn smiled down at her three-year-old son, the image of his father, and tousled his hair.

For a moment she turned her attention to the newsy letter from her mother, hearing more stories about Grandma Brighton's escapades since she moved to Florida and the wonderful news about Anne and her family.

Kathryn sighed and folded the letter, sliding it back into the envelope. She peered at her paperwork and turned off her computer monitor. She would work more later.

She looked around her grandmother's temporary bedroom, conceding that it made a fine office. When she learned Jimmy was on the way—James Tanner, named after his doting grandfather—she'd convinced her boss to allow her to work out of her home with an occasional trip to the office. It had gone well.

A door closed, and Jimmy dropped the book and toddled to the doorway. "Daddy," he cried.

Lucas sailed through the door, scooping his son into his arms. "How's my big boy?"

"Good," Jimmy said, checking his mother's face. "Read to me, Daddy. Please."

Lucas grinned. Jimmy had learned one important lesson. *Please* always reaped reward. "All right, son, but first I have to kiss your mommy."

Lowering Jimmy to the floor, Lucas reached for Kat. She stepped into his arms, treasuring his gentle, loving kiss. "And how's our daughter?" he asked, patting her rounded belly, then bending to kiss her firm bulge.

"Kicking like a mule," she said. "She's the liveliest little lady I know." Memories filled her mind. "Hmm, maybe not." Kathryn picked up her mother's letter. "I've been thinking that Ida might be a nice middle name for our new daughter."

Lucas chuckled and bent down, lifting Jimmy in one arm, then wrapped the other around Kat. "You know, it might be fun to have another Ida around."

* * * * *

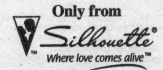

If you enjoyed what you just read,
then we've got an offer you can't resist!

Take 2 bestselling
love stories FREE!

Plus get a FREE surprise gift!

Clip this page and mail it to Silhouette Reader Service™

IN U.S.A.
3010 Walden Ave.
P.O. Box 1867
Buffalo, N.Y. 14240-1867

IN CANADA
P.O. Box 609
Fort Erie, Ontario
L2A 5X3

YES! Please send me 2 free Silhouette Romance® novels and my free surprise gift. After receiving them, if I don't wish to receive anymore, I can return the shipping statement marked cancel. If I don't cancel, I will receive 6 brand-new novels every month, before they're available in stores! In the U.S.A., bill me at the bargain price of $3.15 plus 25¢ shipping and handling per book and applicable sales tax, if any*. In Canada, bill me at the bargain price of $3.50 plus 25¢ shipping and handling per book and applicable taxes**. That's the complete price and a savings of at least 10% off the cover prices—what a great deal! I understand that accepting the 2 free books and gift places me under no obligation ever to buy any books. I can always return a shipment and cancel at any time. Even if I never buy another book from Silhouette, the 2 free books and gift are mine to keep forever.

215 SEN DFNQ
315 SEN DFNR

Name	(PLEASE PRINT)	
Address	Apt.#	
City	State/Prov.	Zip/Postal Code

* Terms and prices subject to change without notice. Sales tax applicable in N.Y.
** Canadian residents will be charged applicable provincial taxes and GST.
All orders subject to approval. Offer limited to one per household and not valid to current Silhouette Romance® subscribers.
® are registered trademarks of Harlequin Enterprises Limited.

SROM01   ©1998 Harlequin Enterprises Limited

SILHOUETTE® MAKES YOU A STAR!

Feel like a star with Silhouette.

We will fly you and a guest to New York City for an exciting weekend stay at a glamorous 5-star hotel. Experience a refreshing day at one of New York's trendiest spas and have your photo taken by a professional. Plus, receive $1,000 U.S. spending money!

**Flowers...long walks...dinner for two...
how does Silhouette Books
make romance come alive for you?**

Send us a script, with 500 words or less, along with visuals (only drawings, magazine cutouts or photographs or combination thereof). Show us how Silhouette Makes Your Love Come Alive. Be creative and have fun. No purchase necessary. All entries must be clearly marked with your name, address and telephone number. All entries will become property of Silhouette and are not returnable. **Contest closes September 28, 2001.**

Please send your entry to: **Silhouette Makes You a Star!**

In U.S.A.
P.O. Box 9069
Buffalo, NY, 14269-9069

In Canada
P.O. Box 637
Fort Erie, ON, L2A 5X3

Look for contest details on the next page, by visiting www.eHarlequin.com or request a copy by sending a self-addressed envelope to the applicable address above. Contest open to Canadian and U.S. residents who are 18 or over. Void where prohibited.

Silhouette®
TM
Where love comes alive™

Our lucky winner's photo will appear in a Silhouette ad. Join the fun!

SRMYAS1

HARLEQUIN "SILHOUETTE MAKES YOU A STAR!" CONTEST 1308
OFFICIAL RULES
NO PURCHASE NECESSARY TO ENTER

1. To enter, follow directions published in the offer to which you are responding. Contest begins June 1, 2001, and ends on September 28, 2001. Entries must be postmarked by September 28, 2001, and received by October 5, 2001. Enter by hand-printing (or typing) on an 8 ½" x 11" piece of paper your name, address (including zip code), contest number/name and attaching a script containing 500 words or less, along with drawings, photographs or magazine cutouts, or combinations thereof (i.e., collage) on no larger than 9" x 12" piece of paper, describing how the Silhouette books make romance come alive for you. Mail via first-class mail to: Harlequin "Silhouette Makes You a Star!" Contest 1308, (in the U.S.) P.O. Box 9069, Buffalo, NY 14269-9069, (in Canada) P.O. Box 637, Fort Erie, Ontario, Canada L2A 5X3. Limit one entry per person, household or organization.

2. Contests will be judged by a panel of members of the Harlequin editorial, marketing and public relations staff. Fifty percent of criteria will be judged against script and fifty percent will be judged against drawing, photographs and/or magazine cutouts. Judging criteria will be based on the following:

   - Sincerity—25%
   - Originality and Creativity—50%
   - Emotionally Compelling—25%

   In the event of a tie, duplicate prizes will be awarded. Decisions of the judges are final.

3. All entries become the property of Torstar Corp. and may be used for future promotional purposes. Entries will not be returned. No responsibility is assumed for lost, late, illegible, incomplete, inaccurate, nondelivered or misdirected mail.

4. Contest open only to residents of the U.S. (except Puerto Rico) and Canada who are 18 years of age or older, and is void wherever prohibited by law; all applicable laws and regulations apply. Any litigation within the Province of Quebec respecting the conduct or organization of a publicity contest may be submitted to the Régie des alcools, des courses et des jeux for a ruling. Any litigation respecting the awarding of a prize may be submitted to the Régie des alcools, des courses et des jeux only for the purpose of helping the parties reach a settlement. Employees and immediate family members of Torstar Corp. and D. L. Blair, Inc., their affiliates, subsidiaries and all other agencies, entities and persons connected with the use, marketing or conduct of this contest are not eligible to enter. Taxes on prizes are the sole responsibility of the winner. Acceptance of any prize offered constitutes permission to use winner's name, photograph or other likeness for the purposes of advertising, trade and promotion on behalf of Torstar Corp., its affiliates and subsidiaries without further compensation to the winner, unless prohibited by law.

5. Winner will be determined no later than November 30, 2001, and will be notified by mail. Winner will be required to sign and return an Affidavit of Eligibility/Release of Liability/Publicity Release form within 15 days after winner notification. Noncompliance within that time period may result in disqualification and an alternative winner may be selected. All travelers must execute a Release of Liability prior to ticketing and must possess required travel documents (e.g., passport, photo ID) where applicable. Trip must be booked by December 31, 2001, and completed within one year of notification. No substitution of prize permitted by winner. Torstar Corp. and D. L. Blair, Inc., their parents, affiliates and subsidiaries are not responsible for errors in printing of contest, entries and/or game pieces. In the event of printing or other errors that may result in unintended prize values or duplication of prizes, all affected game pieces or entries shall be null and void. **Purchase or acceptance of a product offer does not improve your chances of winning.**

6. Prizes: (1) Grand Prize—A 2-night/3-day trip for two (2) to New York City, including round-trip coach air transportation nearest winner's home and hotel accommodations (double occupancy) at The Plaza Hotel, a glamorous afternoon makeover at a trendy New York spa, $1,000 in U.S. spending money and an opportunity to have a professional photo taken and appear in a Silhouette advertisement (approximate retail value: $7,000). (10) Ten Runner-Up Prizes of gift packages (retail value $50 ea.). Prizes consist of only those items listed as part of the prize. Limit one prize per person. Prize is valued in U.S. currency.

7. For the name of the winner (available after December 31, 2001) send a self-addressed, stamped envelope to: Harlequin "Silhouette Makes You a Star!" Contest 1197 Winners, P.O. Box 4200 Blair, NE 68009-4200 or you may access the www.eHarlequin.com Web site through February 28, 2002.

Contest sponsored by Torstar Corp., P.O Box 9042, Buffalo, NY 14269-9042.

SILHOUETTE *Romance*

COMING NEXT MONTH

#1546 THE MISSING MAITLAND—Stella Bagwell
Maitland Maternity: The Prodigal Children
A mysterious man rescued TV reporter Blossom Woodward—and
then kidnapped her! Blossom's nose for news knew there was more to
Larkin the handyman than what he claimed…was he the missing
Maitland they'd been searching for? Only *close* questioning could
uncover the truth…!

#1547 WHEN THE LIGHTS WENT OUT…—Judy Christenberry
Having the Boss's Baby
Scared of small spaces, Sharon Davies turned to a stranger when she
was stranded in an elevator, and got to know him *intimately*. Months
later, she nearly fainted when she met her boss's biggest client. How
could she tell Jack their time in the dark had created a little bundle
of joy?

#1548 WORKING OVERTIME—Raye Morgan
Temporarily sharing a house with a woman and her toddlers awoke
painful memories in Michael Greco, and sharing an office created more
tension! The brooding tycoon tried to avoid Chareen Wolf and her sons,
but eluding the boys was one thing—resisting their alluring mother was
more difficult….

#1549 A GIRL, A GUY AND A LULLABY—Debrah Morris
A friend was all aspiring singer Ryanne Rieger was looking for when
she returned to her hometown broke, disillusioned and pregnant. She
found one in rancher Tom Hunnicutt. But Tom wouldn't be content with
just friends—and could Ryanne ever let herself give more…?

#1550 TEN WAYS TO WIN HER MAN—Beverly Bird
Sparks flew the moment Danielle Harrington and Maxwell Padgett
met. Strong willed and used to getting her own way, Danielle tried
everything she could to make successful and sophisticated Max fall for
her, except the one thing guaranteed to win his heart: being herself!

#1551 BORN TO BE A DAD—Martha Shields
Good Samaritan Rick McNeal became a temporary dad because of an
accident. When Kate Burnett and little Joey needed a home, the lonely
widower opened his door—but would he ever open his heart?

RSCNM0901